The Jadoo
of
Your Love!

I0660065

The Jadoo
of
Your Love!

S.R. Saha

Srishti
PUBLISHERS & DISTRIBUTORS

SRISHTI PUBLISHERS & DISTRIBUTORS
N-16, C. R. Park
New Delhi 110 019
editorial@srishtipublishers.com

First published by
Srishti Publishers & Distributors in 2013

Typeset by EGP at Srishti

ACKNOWLEDGEMENT

This time I need to acknowledge my readers first. The success of my first novel, '*Jab* se you have loved me... *the story of an Airhostess and an IITian*', is only because of all those who have chosen to spend their hard earned money on buying the book. I am indeed grateful to all of them.

Second, I really don't know how to thank them but I simply couldn't have done without their help - my Samsung netbook computer, Windows XP, MS Word, Google, Chrome and Wikipedia.

Third, I must thank my family in particular, and for no particular reason.

Finally, I must express my indebtedness to the team at Srishti for completing the process of publishing this book in record time.

– S.R.Saha

*****

PROLOGUE

Remember Ujani? Well, for the information of those who haven't read 'Jab se you have loved me', she was the heroine of that story, an airhostess with Pan India Airlines. I had intended to write her story, the story of an airhostess. However, things didn't go as per plan. This seems to be always happening with me, '*jo sochta, woh to hota nahin, aur jo hota woh kabhie socha bhi nahin...* whatever I think of never happens, and what happens, I have never thought of that!'

Ujani had quit her job with Pan India Airlines, and devoted all her time to the orphanage she had set up. Her husband Atin flourished in his business while also making a difference to the society. Of course readers of 'Jab se...' know that.

When I met Ujani to pursue her story, it was not the best of times. She was in the family way, and in spite of my prodding, she told me rather bluntly, pointing at her bloated tummy, 'Dada, I don't want you to write a story about me. I don't want my child to read all that you write.' There was a meaningful smirk on her face and I understood what she meant. I was about to tell her that the grand old man of Indian literature, Sardar Khuswant Singh sahib, and the very popular Madam Sobhaa De penned even raunchier stuff, but she cut me short and said, 'Dada, I will send you to someone. You can write his story. It will be no less interesting than that of an airhostess's.'

I was skeptical, and prepared to leave, but she kept insisting.

'Who is he by the way?' I asked, a little annoyed, wondering how to find another airhostess for my next story.

'Anurag Sen,' Ujani had replied.

'Anurag Sen, the famed film director?' I couldn't hide my surprise.

'Yes,' she said with a twinkle in her eyes as Atin entered the living room and exclaimed excitedly on seeing me, '*Arre* Dada, you must stay back tonight. We'll have a party.'

'Some other day,' I told him. Though he looked a bit disappointed, I chose to ignore that. My mind was focused entirely on the subject of my next story. 'Yes, Anurag Sen's story could be interesting. I shall find some airhostess later on,' I thought.

'But will he meet me?' I asked Ujani, sounding uncertain.

'Definitely,' Ujani was confident, and added, 'I shall arrange for that.' I didn't ask her how. I was fully aware of Ujani's capabilities.

The meeting with Anurag Sen took place at his spacious South City apartment, three days later. Here is his amazing story, as told by him.

CHHOTA BACHCHA JAAN KE NA
KOYI AANKH DIKHAANA RE...

As usual, a wave of muffled laughter rippled through the classroom as Professor Gobardhan Dhol was seen at the door. He was one of those rare people, whose very appearance itself tickled one to laugh out loud. He was short, bald, paunchy with a tiny uneven moustache in the cleft between his upper lip and nose. In spite of the suspenders, his trousers always seemed to be on the verge of slipping down. If he ever took to acting in movies or comedy shows, Johnny Lever or Kesto Mukherjee would surely have been out of business.

But appearances can be deceptive and Professor Gobardhan Dhol, who took the 'Fast foods and its effect on the society' class for the second year graduate students of Modern Studies in New Town College in Kolkata, was one of the meanest persons that we had ever come across. Failing a student gave him immense pleasure and he was instrumental in rusticating at least five students in the college in the past one year. But, the reason of his hateful behavior towards the students could not be entirely blamed on his genes alone. In a way, the students had a role to play as well.

Professor Gobardhan Dhol, who was generally referred to as Gobar Dhol, had faced it all – humiliation to physical abuse from the students in myriad forms. In fact, the principal of the college, Dr. Raja Mohan, often lamented as to how these students with such brilliant ideas and perfect execution powers of their mischievous projects came to study in that obscure college and that too subjects which could never get one a job (unless of course one was extremely lucky or had the minister of human resource development as his uncle) and not gotten admission to an IIT!

Much to the frustration of many, even the principal of the college always toed Professor Gobar Dhol's line and never ever confronted him. It was rumored that the college had been built on Professor Gobar Dhol's ancestral property and with his financial assistance, and so he was the final authority on matters concerning disciplining the students, a portfolio that he chose not to delegate to anyone else.

While Professor Gobardhan Dhol's parents couldn't have done much with their family surname Dhol –the ubiquitous double-sided barrel Indian drum -- they couldn't have probably imagined that his impertinent students would be distorting even his name Gobardhan – another name of Lord Krishna-- to just Gobar that meant cow-dung. Unfortunately, he had been a victim of the students' pranks since the beginning of his career as a teacher. He had to endure it all – from a shower of sneezing powder that clouded his office when he had switched on the fan to a live snake carefully placed in the commode of the toilet attached to his office.

Professor Gobar Dhol, who always entered the classroom with a long cane in hand, paused at the door. Though college professors entering classrooms with a cane was certainly an odd sight, it somehow suited him perfectly. The cane served multiple purposes from beating a student mercilessly for a minor mistake to switching on the lights and fans. He never touched any switch board with bare hands after he had got a near fatal electrical shock while switching on the lights in one of the classrooms. Whether it was because of a genuinely faulty switch or a student's trick could never be ascertained, but strangely the same switch never gave shock to anyone after that stray incident.

Professor Gobar Dhol gazed sharply at the arc-shaped classroom that was constructed like a gallery so as to facilitate those sitting behind to have a clear view of the boards and screens on the professor's stage. This type of seating arrangement was advantageous to students, for it was not possible for anyone from the stage to have an accurate idea of who was present and who wasn't. The class was large with an enrolment of over eighty students in it. He focused his attention to certain benches at the back where the trouble-makers generally perched themselves. He wasn't apparently pleased to see a full house that day, and started off his lecture grumpily.

Mote, who always sat beside me, was missing as usual. He could never make it in time to the first class. Mote was also called Motu by some wasn't of course his real name. He was called so by one and all since his school days for his physique. He was plump and his cherubic face reflected a sort of dumb innocence.

৪৩

I had first met Mote on the admission day of our eleventh standard class when he came to join our school from another one. He was caught at the gate by some twelfth standard seniors who found him to be the perfect *murga* to flag off the ragging session with. He was taken to the back of the school for the standard ragging procedures like having to dance without any clothes to the whistling of other boys, to part with all the money he had and so on. I had followed the group to the backyard along with the others to have my share of the fun. I had been studying in that school since first standard and so, even though I was also a fresher to the plus-two classes, I wasn't a victim of ragging at the hands of the seniors. Besides, no one messed with me after I had become the inter-school karate champion while studying in the tenth standard and had always had an improvised *nunchaku* with me in my rucksack. The *nunchaku* was made under my guidance by a local carpenter with the handles of a skipping rope and iron chains purchased from Gariahat market. There had however, been no provocation for taking it out, until then. The *nunchaku* was inspired by none other than the legendary Bruce Lee. Though he belonged to a generation some twenty years before me I considered him to be my guru, following my martial arts teacher who had Bruce Lee's photograph alongside the deities he worshipped. He had shown me, along with his students all of Bruce Lee's movies played on a VCR a number of times, and I never got bored watching them again and again.

After Mote was made to dance for a while in his underwear, with the cheering crowd of about a score of students clapping and shouting in a rhythm twisting the lyrics of a recent hit song making it sound even more vulgar, '*Choli ke peechhe kya hain, chaddhi ke neeche kya hain*'...'one of the twelfth standard bullies pulled down his Jockey brief from behind, exposing his bare bum. Mote held on to his last piece of clothing for life and broke down. He looked around, sprinted a short distance and fell at my feet. 'Help me please,' he pleaded. I don't know what had taken over me then, but a bout of compassion for this innocent, helpless boy prompted me to pull him up and say, 'Don't worry, as long as I am there.' I walked over to where his clothes were lying and picked them up. Mote dressed up as fast as he could and though the other boys were initially stunned at the sudden show of my camaraderie for another eleventh standard student, they didn't quite like an abrupt end to a show when the fun had just begun. The twenty-odd boys surrounded us and told Mote to strip fully while one slapped him. One of the bullies shouted that I too should be made to strip and dance along with Mote for being a spoil-sport. The suggestion was accepted unanimously and the biggest bully, who was in twelfth standard for the past three years for having failed to clear the ISC examinations, came close to me and hit me with a ruler that was in his hand. He shouted the general expletives...*sala, chutia* etc. before vowing to teach me a lesson. Anger gripped me from head to toe and I took out the *nunchaku* from my rucksack in a flash. I made a small prayer to my guru Bruce Lee and took the perfect kung-fu stance, just as he did before taking on the goons outside a Chinese restaurant in a scene from 'Return of the Dragon', a movie that I had watched at least twenty times by then. Though most of the other boys were taken aback by my aggressive posture, big bully and a half-dozen of his friends weren't willing to give up easily. But it took less than a minute for me make a few of them take the ground and writhe in pain. Mote watched me with his eyes almost popping out and mouth wide open as I punched and kicked the other boys with the *nunchaku* in my hand whirling like *Sudarshan Chakra* of Lord Krishna. The boys scooted with the same old hollow warning which all loosing Indians use, '*Baad mein dekh lunga,*'... leaving Mote and myself alone.

From that day, Mote whose real name was Aditya Agarwal, was inseparable from me and always addressed me as, 'Guru.' He sat beside me in the last but one bench of the class that was permanently reserved for us. In a short while, Mote became fully dependent on me for not just protection, but almost everything. I advised him repeatedly that when it came to academic matters, he should consult the other brighter boys. But he didn't pay much heed to that and often sought my guidance just before the examinations.

'Guru, just tell me the portions you are studying,' he would come up with this request, for it was beyond his capability and mine to study everything that was in the syllabus. I studied only a part of all that we were told to study and did okay if my postulations came correct, else had to try for 'hall collection' to jot down some answers to those questions that seemed Greek to me. After failing in a number of tests, I had repeatedly asked Mote to part ways. I had told him angrily, '*Sala* Mote, if you keep following me, you'll fail in the board examinations as well.'

But Mote was unperturbed and used to say smiling stupidly munching something or the other, 'Guru if you fail, I have no problem failing either.' That was in a way flattering, but as the twelfth standard board examinations drew near, I started to get the jitters.

All the teachers were united in their views that the examinations results following that year would decide as to who would become an engineer, a doctor, an accountant or an auto-rickshaw driver or a delivery boy. No, they did not mention the millions of other decent professions that one could choose from. They had segregated the class into two imaginary sections, one that would take up the coveted professions and would earn a lot of money and respect from the society, while the other would have to accept an ignoble existence. Obviously, Mote and I were placed in the second group.

But in spite of the threat from the teachers, the prospects of leading the life of a delivery boy looming large and in contrast the optimism of my parents that I would be someone successful like one of my elder cousins who was working for IBM after graduating from IIT, Delhi somewhere deep inside, I knew how much I tried, I couldn't get an admission into an engineering or medical college. Sadly, no one realised that everyone had his limitations. Not everyone could climb the Everest, not everyone could be Amartya Sen, not everyone could influence the masses like Lalooji and not everyone could shed clothes like Zeenat Aman or Helen (Bipasa Basu and Mallika Sherawat weren't around then!) and yet look glamorous.

For Mote, life wasn't as miserable as mine. His father owned a chain of sweetmeat shops in Kolkata where business was brisk and he was more or less expected to look after the family business after he graduated. For him, a degree in the Marwari household would have added sheen to the wealth they already possessed and that is what he strove for. Things were different for me. My father was a scientist at the Bose Institute and my mother a school teacher who taught mathematics in South Point High School. They expected me to become a an engineer and reminded me at least a dozen times that they wouldn't be able to show their faces to the neighborhood or in the relatives circle if I couldn't get admission into a prestigious college, at least the Jadavpur University or the Regional Engineering Colleges, if not an IIT. I was fed up of their constant advice and their obsession with finding the right teacher and coaching class for me. I ended up running from one tutorial home to another, learning nothing. Sigh! Those days '3 Idiots' was not released to enlighten the parent community on the futility of conventional education. I have my doubts though if my parents would have seen the movie, for they despised Hindi cinema, something they thought ought to be banned for it did nothing other than corrupting young minds. I, however, loved cinema and wouldn't miss an opportunity to watch a film by bunking some class or the other.

Besides cinema, sports interested me very much and I played a lot ... football, cricket, and tennis – anything. Though I loved playing more than studying, I however very well knew I couldn't be another Sunil Gavaskar or Vijay Amritraj to make a living out of sports, a sad fact that was reminded again and again by my parents and teachers. I loved swimming too, and never lost any opportunity to jump into a pool. Swimming relaxed me a lot as my worries and anger seemed to be swept away by the waves and splashes of water. Mote, who didn't know swimming and had no intentions of learning it either, used to run along the poolside, cheering me during the occasional races in which I used to participate.

Much to the disappointment of my parents, I couldn't crack any of the JEEs that I had attempted. My misery was compounded by the fact that a close cousin, my own mother's own sister's own son, secured admission to IIT, Kharagpur. I ran around with my modest twelfth standard mark-sheet from college to college for admission, with Mote in tow. Mote's marks were worse and he had just managed to pass the ISC examination by a slim margin. But his oversized parents, Mr. Brajesh Agarwal and Mrs. Geeta Agarwal, were all smiles for their son having managed to pass the board examinations in the first attempt, a feat that was a rarity in their family. Mote's younger sister Aditi, who defied all laws of genetics and was slim, fair and beautiful distributed sweets amongst her friends for her *bhaiya*'s success in the board examinations.

In my household, there was silence as if someone had died. But it was soon broken with the bickering and quarrelling between my parents - father putting the blame on my mother and vice versa

--- and finally the duo teaming up to shout at me. I hated being at home and tried to spend as much time as possible outside.

'He can only hog like a pig,' mother would start at dinnertime. 'Let him learn how to polish shoes. I will buy him a stand to take to the Howrah station. Before that he can rub some of that black polish on my face.' Father was no less a competition to mother in his stinging remarks. Being the only son made matters worse and though I knew I had let them down, I could do nothing about that.

To be honest, I just couldn't remember the structure of bromofluromethane that was asked in the chemistry section of one of the JEE papers or answer anything about Stephan- Boltzmann law that was asked in the Physics paper of another entrance test. My salute to those who could really cross these hurdles like tigers jumping through fire rings in a circus. They are indeed tigers in this circus of the competitive world.

'Guru,' Mote had asked me, gobbling up a chicken roll (though strictly a vegetarian at home, Mote was an eager non-vegetarian outside), 'Shall we get admission to any college at all?' We had just been shown the door by the clerk of the college that we had last ventured into to find out if there were any vacant seats. Seeing my mark-sheet, he had flung it out and had said gruffly, 'Have you checked the marks of the student who had been taken in last?'

'Yes Sir,' I had replied.

'How much?' He had asked.

'Eighty seven percent.' I had mumbled.

'Yours?' He had thundered.

'Forty-five Sir,' I had replied with a sigh. The conversation ended there.

Mote hadn't taken the trouble of taking out his mark-sheet from the folder that he was carrying but helped me in picking up mine from the floor. We had left the college and as usual Mote's eyes searched for something to eat. He could have been a detective for he had this exceptional ability to sniff out food outlets at any part of the city. His pockets were always full too with generous pocket-money being doled out by his loving parents every now and then. He, however chose to travel by public transport with me, after I had firmly declined his offer of moving around in one of his family's cars.

Mote's question made the chicken roll taste like chopped grass wrapped in *sal* leaf (though I had never tasted a *sal* leaf, or for that matter grass, the simile came to my mind anyway) but quickly gobbled it nevertheless. Not getting an entry into any college was indeed a very frightening thought.

However, after a few days we did get admission to the newly founded New Town College in the course titled 'Modern Studies' leading to a Bachelor's degree.

'B.A' or 'B.Sc.'? I had asked the clerk after he had taken the rather large amount of money that my parents had grudgingly given. They had no choice either – a college degree if they had given the money, no further education for their only son if they hadn't.

'Of course B.Sc.' He had said and added, 'As soon as the university approves the course.'

I hadn't asked him as to what happened if the course was not approved, for I didn't want to spoil my mood over some negative reply.

Mote enrolled himself for the same course, albeit the fact that his father was able to get him an admission into a hotel management course in Bangalore. Though they would have been happy to see Mote with a degree in hotel management, they never pressurised their son over his choice of college or course.

I was relieved to find over eighty students in the class and was glad to know that there were many like Mote and me who couldn't get admission to IITs or the Calcutta Medical College or any other good colleges like Presidency or Lady Brabourne or St. Xavier's. The New Town College had a huge campus and offered other courses too, like Economics, Bio Sciences, Anthropology, Mathematics and so on. Mote and me, with our modest marks in the board examinations however, were not eligible for those courses which already having been approved by the University of Calcutta were much in demand by students with better scores.

First year went off like a breeze. Mote and I occupied the last but one row in the class, just as we did in school and didn't mix up with the other boys and girls of the class much. There were more girls in the class, and most of the boys did not attend classes regularly. We commuted from home, for hostel rooms were in short supply and given only to students second year onwards. A few girls tried to make friends with me, but beyond a certain point, I didn't drag those friendships. I knew being friendly with girls would mean having to spend money, something that I could ill-afford those days. That was an era when going Dutch, particularly when accompanying a girl to a restaurant or a movie wasn't in fashion. The girls poked and made fun of Mote and that was one more reason why I couldn't be too friendly with them.

'Hey Mote,' one of the girls would giggle and tickle Mote's paunch. Mote would become red with anger and say, 'I am not Mote, I am Aditya.' That only brought more laughter and taunts from the other girls in the group, which Mote did not enjoy at all.

But life changed in the second year.

৪০

On that day, Mote had sneaked into the classroom when Professor Gobar Dhol had gone out ostensibly for a pee. Mote, unlike as on other days when he was cool and with some grub in hand, walked in empty handed and seemingly excited. 'Guru,' he said in a whisper, 'Have some news.' I hushed him up for I could see Professor Gobar Dhol's shadow at the doors. Anyway, Mote's news was generally about some new blue film that his friendly neighborhood video parlour owner had added in his stock. I was almost sure that he was going to tell me about the latest releases, '*Bang Bang in Bangladesh*' or '*Chham Chham Chhamiya*,' and so I was in no hurry in listening to what Mote had to say.

Professor Gobar Dhol started off again to talk at length how harmful fast food, particularly street food could be. Neither Mote nor I liked the topic, as we practically lived on street food, but we pretended to jot down his notes frantically. Mote was certainly agitated and could not concentrate on the lecture. I felt that to be somewhat odd. Even if the new film was a rocker like the all-time great about two lovers, who filmed themselves during a pre-marital romp which got leaked while the guy was trying to transfer the content from the camera to a VHS cassette, Mote shouldn't have been that excited. I waited for the class to get over to find out what was bothering him. However, it took a little longer than usual. As soon as Professor Gobar Dhol had exited, the Dean entered the classroom. He was a nice and jovial guy, and it seemed that he was waiting outside for Professor Gobar Dhol's lecture to get over.

'I have an announcement to make,' he declared quite dramatically. Mote and I, who had risen from our seats, sat down again. What he said made the class to break into a big cheerful roar. He informed us that a picnic for all first and second year students was being arranged and those interested could enroll themselves with the student councilors by paying a small fee.

'So, Mote, what's up?' I asked him in the corner of a corridor as soon as we got out of the classroom.

'Guru, I'll tell you later, I am not feeling well, please excuse me today.' Mote did a U-turn from his initial stance about disclosing something in the class and left in a hurry. I got a bit worried about him. No, he wasn't looking physically unwell. I wondered what could have happened to him. There were no more classes and I too left the college premises for home. As I headed for the bus stop, I saw a group of girls giggling and chatting. I took a cursory glance at them. 'First year students', I concluded. Usually, I didn't look up at girls, as like Mote, I too suffered from an undecipherable inferiority complex. Mote was uncomfortable with girls, for he knew they looked upon him as an object for making fun. I was because I never had any money other than the bus fare in my pocket. My parents, amongst many other wrong conceptions that they possessed, thought that money spoilt young people. Mote had at times told me, 'Guru, you are the most handsome guy in the class, yet no girlfriends?' I snubbed him off trying to be macho not quite disclosing the real reason for not trying to be friendly with girls.

I was walking away, but turned my head once more in the direction of the girls. A tall, fair girl, with stunning looks caught my eye. For a moment I lost my senses, as lines from an unforgettable Mohammed Rafi song played back in my mind, '....*taarif karu kya uski jisne tumhe banaya...* '.Indeed I didn't know how do I praise the lord who had made her so beautiful. But that emotional entrapment was momentary as I sighed and jumped on a moving bus.

Mote remained absent from classes for the next couple of days. When he rejoined, I could notice a transformation in him. He was not quite his old self. The exuberance in him was missing and he seemed to have become pensive overnight. This was getting serious and at the first opportunity I could pin him, I took him to a secluded corner behind a large banyan tree in the campus to know exactly what had happened.

'Mote, tell me what has happened to you.' I was authoritative. Mote was hesitant first, a trait that I had noticed in him for the first time in my life. But he spilled the beans. What he said made me gasp.

'Guru, I think I am in love.' He said after a pregnant pause.

'Love?' I was thunderstruck. And that too Mote…oh no! I burst into laughter.

Mote seemed hurt, but fell silent. I was going to ask him the details, being extremely curious to know of the girl who chose Mote as her lover. Of course, for any girl, Mote wouldn't have been a bad choice at all. He came from a rich family, and if his weight could be ignored, he was not bad looking at all.

But then Mote mumbled, 'Guru I want to meet that lady. She has given me her address. He fished out a crumpled piece of paper on which it was written in a wavy feminine and charming handwriting – *House No. 10, Professors' Colony.*

'Oh, some professor's daughter or niece,' I concluded and said, 'Mote, keep me away from all these.' There was definite risk in those attempts. I couldn't be in the firing line of any professor. If anything happened to Mote, he had his business to fall back upon, but I had to secure a degree to be eligible to sell myself in the job market. No, I couldn't accompany Mote. Mote fell silent and after a while, seeing his sad face, I couldn't stick to my resolution and said, 'Ok, I'll come with you, but tell me how it all happened.'

Mote narrated the incident.

As he was coming for college for an early morning additional class, he had taken the route from behind the campus. It was a deserted road which not many people used and one got the feeling that he was inside a forest. There he came across a helpless lady in front of a stationary Fiat car. When Mote saw her, she had called him and asked, 'Can you help me please? I'm unable to start the car.'

Mote had opened the bonnet and found that the lead from the battery had gotten disconnected, a common snag in those cars. Mote had good knowledge about cars since his family owned a number of them. Mote fixed it in no time, and started the car. The lady then had not only thanked him but also gave her address along with extending an invitation to visit her house.

'Oh, this is the mother of all love-at-first-sight stories,' I said with a chuckle.

Mote seemed to be a bit hurt at my taunt and got lost in thoughts when I asked him, 'Well what makes you think that the lady is in love with you as well?'

'No, it's not that kind of love,' Mote tried to defend himself, 'There is something in that lady that is attracting me like a magnet.'

'Magnet?' Oh!' I couldn't help exclaiming. Mote kept silent.

Somewhat reluctantly, I agreed to Mote's request of accompanying him to the lady's house the next evening. That day classes had gotten over earlier than usual, as Professor Dhol had been away. It was learnt that he had gone to Delhi for some work. Mote had brought a Honda SUV from his father's fleet of cars and sitting beside him, I asked, 'Mote are you sure that you want to go there?' Mote didn't say anything but nodded in the affirmative. I could make out that he was determined to meet the lady as he drove straight into the Professors' Colony without uttering a single word. Finding house no. 10 wasn't difficult at all. While Mote parked the car a short distance away, I got down and went close to the bungalow that displayed '10' on one of the pillars of the front gate. But as I neared the green wooden gate, I froze. By then Mote had come beside me and he too seemed to have got the shock of his life. I looked up at him and gestured with my eyes to turn around and scoot. That would have been the best thing to do in those circumstances for the marble plaque fitted right beside the gate displayed in black Gothic italics, 'Prof. G.Dhol.'

Mote stood still for a while, unable to decide what to do, but as I started heading towards the car, he followed me. But immediately thereafter we heard a sweet voice from behind, 'Hi Aditya, come in, what a pleasant surprise.' Mote turned around and so did I. A very attractive fair lady in sleeveless blouse and a blue and yellow sari waved at us from the balcony. She vanished for a moment, only to come back and open the front door. We were at our wit's end. I tried to mumble, 'some other day, ma'am, actually we were just passing your bungalow,' but Mote had already started to tail her and I had no choice but to follow them as well.

She ushered us in to a tastefully done up living room, and disappeared for a while after seating us. She came back with a decorated tray with an exquisite bone china tea set along with some mouthwatering cookies on a plate. She kept it gently on the coffee table in front of the sofa on which we sat. She poured the tea into the cups and asked, 'Sugar? Milk?' We were so awestruck that we stammered even answering that. Yes, I had to admit that the lady was very elegant, besides being stunningly beautiful. But there was an aura of sadness around her that did not skip my eyes.

'I am Adwitia, Professor Dhol's wife,' she introduced herself to us. I had an instant hiccup. I could never imagine that the old haggard would have such a beautiful young wife. Mote appeared to be devastated but somewhat managed to compose himself, when the lady asked, 'Aren't you feeling well?' Thereafter, I didn't wait for long and excused myself out as soon as I finished my cup of tea. Mote had no other option than to come out with me.

'Do come again,' she said with earnestness as she bid us 'good-bye'.

Though I responded, 'Certainly ma'am,' I thought, 'never again in my lifetime.'

On our way back, seated beside Mote in the SUV, I said with a sigh, 'Wrong number, you've to forget her, she's Professor Gobardhan Dhol's wife after all. ' And then I added, 'She's so young, I first thought her to be Gobar Dhol's daughter.' I warned Mote, 'Never ever make any attempt to meet her again. It will be as suicidal as jumping from the top deck of the Shaheed Minar.'

I don't know why 'Shaheed Minar' came to my mind of all the tall buildings. May be it was because of its name. Jumping from the 'Shaheed Minar' over spurned love would make one the perfect martyr. I wondered stupidly if Sir David Ochterlony, when he had erected this monument at the heart of Calcutta in 1825 to commemorate both his successful defense of Delhi against the Marathas in 1804 and the victory of the East India Company's armed forces over the Gurkhas in the Anglo-Nepalese War, could have ever imagined it being renamed 'Shaheed or Martyrs' Monument' someday.

All the way back Mote did not speak a word.

৪০

A few days later I took Mote to an isolated place in the campus to lecture him a bit as I noticed him sulking since the day of our meeting Mrs. Dhol. But before I could begin, a small crowd of boys and girls spotted us. They came closer and handed out a leaflet about the picnic that was to take place the next day. They informed us that there would be four buses, two each for first and second year students which would head for the picnic spot located somewhere near the Sunderbans, a beautiful scenic place on the bank of a river. The buses would leave the college at six o'clock in the morning sharp and we could also take it from certain points on the way; the additional information was provided by one of the organisers in the team, who also warned us, 'Don't be late. We won't be waiting for anyone.'

Mote and I nodded in agreement as the boisterous group moved on to pass on picnic related information to the other boys and girls. I checked the route map of the buses and found that they would pass through spots close to our homes. I skipped the counselling of Mote over his lost lady love, as I had intended and went into discussing the picnic. I advised Mote to get up on the last bus meant for second year students from the bus stop near his home. 'It should be there by 6.30, set the alarm to get up for 5.30 positively,' I instructed Mote.

When I boarded the bus the next morning, I was doubtful if Mote would be there, for falling in love I knew made one act in the most foolish ways. I didn't know what it would do to Mote, who was stupid anyway. But much to my relief, Mote was there occupying an aisle seat towards the end of the bus with the window seat being vacant. The usual glee on seeing me flashed across his face as he hailed me. I took the seat beside him and said, 'Thanks Mote.' Mote let out a disapproving snarl, but I found that it was not in response to my utterance but because he spotted the most irritating and over-smart girl of our class taking up the mike. Like any bus meant for fun trips, this too was fitted with a karaoke system. The girl, who won some Miss Birati (a suburb of Calcutta) contest and anchored a few programs on local TV channels, had already developed an attitude of that of Raveena Tandon. She sang a few lines in her croaky voice and declared that there would be an *Antakshari* contest between those sitting on the left side of the bus and with those on the right side. There was a wave of big cheer as everyone got enthused over this. The first lines of various film songs started pouring in from amateurish voices. We kept silent, with me choosing to look outside the window as the grey cityscape was fading out, making way for the soothing green of paddy fields, and Mote closing his eyes, trying to sleep. One of the songs ended with '*sach*', and then there was this menacing announcement by the anchor, 'Ch...ch... now Mr. Mote will sing a song with ch...' She giggled and smirked and I could clearly make out that she was rehearsing the lines to heckle Mote. She seemed almost certain that Mote would decline her invitation or perhaps make a feeble attempt to sing a few lines that would resemble a nursery rhyme. She would then use Mote's failure to gain some more mileage in her 'showing-off'. Some people feel it's a laudable act to taunt and jeer someone else and she was one of them. I sighed and involuntarily tapped my forehead with my left hand palm, for I could almost visualise what was going to happen.

The crowd in the bus burst into a loud roar sensing an opportunity to have some more fun at the cost of Mote. Mote had opened his eyes by then and looked to be wide awake. He took the mike and turned to me. I raised my right hand thumb and Mote broke into a song beginning with 'Ch...' Within a few seconds, there was absolute silence in the bus except for Mote's sonorous voice that filled up the entire space even drowning the engine's hum. After a few lines of '*Chala jaata hun kisike dhun mein'* the evergreen Kishore Kumar's song from the unforgettable Rajesh Khanna movie '*Mere Jeevan Saathi*', Mote handed over the mike to another boy in accordance with the rules of the game of *Antakshari*. But the boy returned the mike to Mote as everyone shouted, 'Continue, continue…'

Mote took back the mike and continued to complete the song, '*milan ki maasti bhari aankho mein...* as I winked at him. The over-smart girl sulked and took a seat, anger over an unexpected defeat writ large on her face as she was no longer the cynosure of the crowd. She was surely regretting her decision of inviting Mote to sing. Mote couldn't stop after the song was as huge uproars of 'one more', 'one more,' shouts filled the bus. After that it was Mote all the way to the picnic spot as he kept singing one song after another on popular demand.

I sighed once again. That Mote was a fabulous singer was no longer a secret which only I knew.

******

2

EHLA NASHA, PEHLA HUMMAR...

The picnic spot was beautiful on a barren land with the river on one side and a forest on the other. After getting down from the bus, Mote was dragged by his newfound fans to another spot where hot fish fries were being served on paper plates. I didn't know if it was for the adulation or the fish fries that Mote chose to accompany them. But I drifted away wandering off towards the forest.

It was not dense or dark inside, the forest comprising mainly of small trees and bushes. There was no one around, and I found the right spot for a piss. My bladder was already bursting after several rounds of soft drinks, tea and water on the long bus journey and I took no time in opening my fly to let my member out.

However, midway between my act, I was startled by a rustle and was totally shocked to see the beautiful girl whom I had spotted the day before staring right at me. Angry over the interruption I yelled, 'Hey, what are you doing here?'

'Shouldn't I be asking you that question,' she answered my question with another but continued with wide open eyes, 'Oh! I can see what you are doing.' She stopped for a while, perhaps shocked at the suddenness of the situation having to confront me in a place where she hadn't expected any intrusion.

I hollered again, 'Who's told you to come here?'

She had quickly gotten to her normal self and retorted, 'Aha, do I need to take anyone's permission to come here? And anyway I came here chasing a butterfly.'

'Butterfly?' I wondered loudly.

'Yes,' she replied and said, 'and if you have finished with that, you can put it inside,' pointing at my crotch with her forefinger. I then realised with utter embarrassment that all this while I was arguing with the girl with my 'member' jutting out of my pants. I quickly zipped up and shouted, 'Now get out of here.'

'Ha, first you do something that you ought to be ashamed of, and then scream at someone else,' she said with scorn and ran off, presumably after spotting another butterfly.

I wanted to carry on with my argument that pissing outdoors was the right of Indian men, but she was gone in a flash. I moved on wondering if pissing in the open was actually a right of Indian men. I ambled towards the river. I sat down on the bank watching small boats oared by young boys float around. One boy came close to the bank and asked me if I wanted a ride. I declined the offer and he steered away. The ambience and the atmosphere made me to get over the embarrassment that I had faced a little while back and made me feel good. I started humming a Tagore song in a tune that would have certainly shocked the greatest bard ever. But there was no around to listen to me and the setting was perfect to stimulate any Bengali into singing, '*Ogo nodi apon bege pagol para…*' (O, the river that flows unmindful of its own buoyant ways)'. I looked around and saw that beautiful girl with whom my first meeting was in a rather 'forgettable' situation, sitting on the river bank just a little distance away. She hadn't noticed me, but seemed as if she was humming some tune as well. I couldn't take my eyes off her attractive figure that resembled the crescent moon against the backdrop of a meandering river. I thought of going to her and apologising, but scuttled the idea. I moved further away and sat behind a rock where she couldn't spot me, but I could see her.

But my peaceful sojourn amidst nature got a sudden break. A group of noisy boys along with Mote came to the river bank. 'We'll have a cruise in the river on a boat,' they shouted in unison. A boat was summoned and in spite of Mote's resistance, the boys persuaded him to board it. Mote was visibly scared, for as I had said earlier, he didn't know a bit of swimming. Seeing me, Mote begged me to come with them, but the boat was already full. I chose to watch them from the bank. The boat quickly moved towards the middle of the river, with the boys singing and enjoying themselves thoroughly. Then I couldn't fathom what exactly happened, but heard a deafening yell and watched with horror as the boat capsized. I lost no time and in fraction of a second, dived into the water and swam close to the boat. I could just spot Mote's head popping up momentarily as he desperately threw his arms and legs to keep afloat. I managed to catch him by his hair and drag him to the shore. I did all that I had learnt from the swimming coach to resurrect Mote and to my great relief, he responded as I pressed his stomach to expel the water. He came back to his senses. Thankfully, all the other boys who were on that boat swam ashore and none were hurt.

'Am I in heaven?' He mumbled opening his eyes and seeing the beautiful, butterfly-chasing girl doing her bit to help him out. But then seeing me, he closed his eyes again and said, 'No, I am still alive.'

Mote was in shock and I accompanied him to a nearby hospital where the doctors declared him to be fit. I had convinced others to carry on with the picnic, since Mote was fine. There was no point in spoiling their fun. We were in no mood to join them and left for home. I could have been mistaken, but as we left, the butterfly-chasing girl looked up at me and I could see in place of anger and hatred a glint of appreciation in her eyes. I had come to know her name by then - Urmi.

On the way back, Mote held my hand and said emotionally, 'Guru, I'll be ever grateful to you. You have saved my life.'

ଌ

College life went on as usual the next day onwards, except the fact that the day after, Urmi, having spotted me in the college canteen came over, pulled out a chair and sat down in front of me. I was having a plate of *samosas* and a cup of tea alone, for Mote who usually accompanied me to the canteen had bunked college that day. In fact, in spite of my lecturing him on and off on the importance of attending classes regularly, there was a perceivable change in his behavior. He was often absent from college and kept evading my questions about his whereabouts.

'You are a good swimmer', she started off with a flattering line at which I just nodded stupidly. I mentally searched for lines to carry on with the conversation and finally after a pause pushed my plate of two *samosas* towards her and said, 'Would you like to have a bite?' Thankfully, I hadn't had a dig at them till then. She declined the offer, but chatted with me for a while. I felt somewhat ashamed to tell her that I was in my second year of Modern Studies, when I learnt that she was in her first year, studying a more respectable Economics Honours.

That night she kept coming back in my dreams, mostly as Neetu Singh in some movie in which I was Rishi Kapoor crooning '*ek main aur ek tu…*'. I woke up with a sigh and brushed aside any thought of her. I reminded myself to remain within my *aukat,* a weighty word which has liberal usage in Hindi movies and not to even think of trying to reach out for the moon.

The fact that a four-week long vacation followed soon, also helped in erasing Urmi from my mind to an extent. During the vacation, I took up a job as a waiter in a small restaurant. I had lied to the owner that I had dropped out of college, or else he wouldn't have employed anyone for a month. Though not quite noble, I enjoyed the work and found out that with the tips, which were at times quite generous from rich diners, the earnings were not bad. During this month, I had quite lost contact with Mote. A little surprising, for there was a time when Mote made sure to call me up once every day on the landline phone that was there at my home. Of course, forget Face book as those were the days when a mobile phone in hand still made a style statement. It was out of bounds for poor students like me, and one could easily not keep in touch with others if he chose to.

I hadn't thought of meeting Urmi during the vacations, but coincidentally we met and in rather extraordinary circumstances.

That evening the restaurant was shut a little earlier as news of some protest close to the location was being reported on TV and there were no customers. I walked up to the bus stop, where many people were standing. One of the commuters informed me that no buses were plying and they had been waiting for an hour. I started walking towards my home, about four kilometers from that place. As I was ambling down, I came close to the place where the road had been blocked. I wanted to avoid it, but it was on my way. I saw buses and other vehicles caught in a thick jam. I walked down the footpath crossing the few hundred men and women with red flags, squatting on the road and shouting slogans. I couldn't make out what their demands were and chose not to listen to them either.

I had walked down the road and unexpectedly spotted Urmi at a distance, coming out of a taxi. She looked lost and puzzled, may be her patience had worn out, forcing her to get off the stuffy taxi. She started trudging into the opposite direction as mine. I crossed the road just to say 'Hi' to her, but she had walked a little further along the footpath and I was just a few yards behind her. She hadn't spotted me and just as I was going to call out her name, I heard a commotion right behind. I turned my back to watch in horror that horse-mounted policemen who were waiting in the dark had started *lathi*-charging to disperse off the crowd. Since the roads were all blocked, a few horses had started trotting on the same footpath as we were walking and one of them had suddenly increased pace and came close to me. I quickly moved towards the railing on the side of the footpath as the horse crossed me. Then, shockingly, I realised that Urmi was walking at her own pace, oblivious of the horse right behind her. I shrieked and ran as fast as I could, overtaking the horse and in the nick of time pulled her towards the railing as the horse darted past us with a few inches to spare. Urmi clung to me in fear and looking up, when she realised that it was me, she heaved a sigh of relief. Oddly, she didn't move away immediately, but held on to me tightly for some more time. When she came back to her senses, she said, 'Thank you,' still trembling.

This time I played my cards right and asked her, 'Should I accompany you to your home.' Her eyes lit up and she said, 'I hope that wouldn't bother you.'

'No, no, not at all,' I said like any young man with the right sexual orientation would. Her house wasn't far off and I dropped her off in front of a beautiful white bungalow. She repeatedly thanked me and on my way back, it dawned on to me that all the way Urmi had held on to my hand. It felt good.

After the college re-opened, my friendship with Urmi grew and perhaps it was so destined. I started enjoying being with her and which young man wouldn't in the company of such a beautiful young lady?

It was perhaps the beginning of an affair of a lifetime.

*****

3

NA RAHA, PYAR PYAR NA RAHA...

As I got more involved with Urmi, Mote drifted away from me. He wasn't a regular in the class anyway, but those days I hardly ever saw him. He had taken different electives and most of our classes were held at different times and in different halls. Occasionally though, when I did meet him, I marveled at the change. He was no longer the Mote that I knew, but had metamorphosed into a smartly dressed young man with six-pack abs. I really couldn't fathom what brought about this change and that too so fast; for I was certain that he never went to meet his first love, after knowing that she was the wife of the person whom we were terrified of. It was so repulsive even to think of falling in love with a professor's wife, and I thought Mote felt exactly as I did.

I had by then moved into a campus hostel, a relief that I was looking forward to every day since joining college. I didn't like going back home to the same old taunts of my parents that they would have to feed me throughout their lifetime. It got worse with the news of anyone in the relation or neighborhood having excelled in studies by securing good marks in some examination, obtaining a scholarship and so on. I could somehow convince my parents of longer study hours, and a possibility of changing over to the Electronics stream from Modern Studies if I did well in the semester examination. They had reluctantly agreed, though skeptical of my abilities to change over to Electronics stream but not quite rejecting it out rightly. In a way they were fools for even partially believing me. After all, I never had the ability to study Electronics, a subject meant for brainy students, something that they should have known. But then, hope makes one to believe in many things which can never become a reality.

Hostel life gave me the freedom I was craving for. In the four-in-one enclosure dorm type hostel room, two of my roommates were commerce students and kept mostly to themselves. The other guy, an Electronics Sciences third year fellow acted as if he was the next Robert Boyce (well, he is the founder of microprocessor company Intel and I like most of you didn't know that until I heard about him in a quiz contest). This particular room-mate of mine was an irritant, and though I did not make my feelings towards him public, I just despised him. He had put up a barricade around the space he was allotted with plywood panels secluding his bed and his study table. I didn't know what he did, but that he kept awake till the wee hours was evident. I didn't talk to him much; neither did the other boys in the room.

College campus rumors were another thing that we savoured, and it felt good to come across tongues wagging over the most beautiful girl in the campus dating me. Not only in my own eyes was Urmi beautiful, for to every person in love, his lady is obviously the most beautiful girl in the world, but a campus magazine had reported her to be the most attractive and coveted girl after having been voted by some couple of thousand students across all classes.

At the same time, another rumor was doing the rounds. There was a dilapidated temple complex just outside the college campus in a desolate place, where nobody used to go. The legend of human sacrifice in that temple was well known, but no one really bothered about that. But that ghosts were haunting the place was a new addition.

'I swear,' the cherubic guy of first year said rather dramatically in the canteen, 'I could hear some strange noises from there when I was passing.'

'When did it happen?' a girl asked.

'Very early in the morning, yesterday,' he said, emphasising that he was absolutely sure of someone's presence in that temple. Though not many seemed to believe his story, he promised to prove the presence of ghosts in the temple and left.

I saw that same guy talking to the geek of my room as I was entering the hostel that evening. I heard that the boy was excitedly narrating the ghost story to him. I expected the geek to brush it away, but on the contrary I saw him to be all ears.

That night, the geek in my room kept awake throughout, and when I got up in the morning he was still working on something. Wires and other gadgets were spread out on his table and I couldn't help querying him, 'Project work?'

'Sort of,' he let out an irksome chuckle. I had never liked this guy and got even more annoyed at the manner he spoke and was moving away, when he added, 'Ghost busting project,' and laughed out loud. I didn't pay any attention to him and went off for my classes.

A couple of days later, late in the evening, the geek came to the room excitedly. He had with him a boxful of gadgets and was being helped by that second year, baby-faced guy who had broken the news of the ghost in the temple.

'Guys,' he spoke in a dramatic fashion. Three of us who were studying for our examinations looked up.

'Guys, I think I have solved the ghost in the temple mystery,' he said, the dramatic tone in his voice intact.

The other two boys became curious, and so did I. The cherubic second year guy perched himself on the bed of the geek. He was so excited that his plump cheeks had become tomato-red. We watched the geek with intent, as he set up his equipment. Soon, on the screen of a TV set that had its back open pictures started getting displayed. He adjusted something and the pictures became crystal clear. Yes, it was a video-recording of the inside of the temple. There was nothing in view for a while, and we listened to him as to how he had set up a hidden camera, with a battery that beamed video wirelessly to the electronics lab that he had recorded on a sophisticated recorder. But even after a fairly long period of bragging, there was no activity on the screen.

'Looks like there is no ghost,' one of the boys commented.

I too was going to comment on similar lines, but then some action started on the screen. What I saw made me speechless. I was petrified.

I saw Mote along with Mrs. Dhol entering the deserted temple. It was a short film in a sense that it took only a few minutes from the frenzied kissing to Mote throwing off a condom, pulling up his pants and zipping up the fly. The lady was in sari, which she had just lifted up and bent forward to facilitate Mote to enter from behind, and it took just a fraction of a second for her to drop it down after the act. They left the temple as hurriedly as they had come. Naturally, no one in their position could risk being there for long.

'I have seen the guy in college, but who's the woman?' One of the boys queried along with a request for a re-run of the ultimate sting operation, the mother of all reality shows. The geek had taken out a tiny cassette from a camera and said in a triumphant tone, 'I'll make copies of this video and distribute throughout the college.' The cherubic guy seconded his declaration. I was in a trance and asked, 'Is this the only copy?'

'Right now, yes, but it won't be in another hour or so.' He said with a menacing chuckle. In a flash I sprang into action and snatched the cassette from his hand along with a perfectly timed jab on his chin. He was stunned, and so were the other boys. I caught the collar of the cherubic guy and ordered him to leave immediately along with a threat, 'If anyone in the college comes to know about this, you are finished.' Then I issued similar threats to the other boys and marched out of the room.

Ambers of anger was burning inside me as I ran to the hostel paid-phone booth. But to my frustration, I found that I didn't have a single one rupee coin with me. In a rage, I banged on the tin box on which the phone was mounted, and to my surprise a number of coins dropped out on the metallic basin emitting those tangs and clangs that startled me. I picked up one coin, inserted it into the slot and started dialing. It was going to be morning in a couple of hours, when I had woken up Mote from his sleep. He was obviously very startled to get a call from me at that hour.

'*Sala* Mote, come to the temple outside the campus immediately,' I yelled and left the receiver. I paced outside the temple impatiently wondering if Mote would come at all. It was still dark, but the first signs of the night fading away appeared after a while. But Mote did arrive shortly in a swanky car which he drove himself. As soon as he got down, I went close to him and slapped him hard on his face. He was taken aback but defended himself. He was not the same Mote and I knew I wouldn't be able to win this time around if a fight broke out.

'What have I done, Anurag?' Mote asked. For the first time in my life he had addressed to me by my name and not 'Guru'.

'What have you done?' I shouted followed by a barrage of expletives, '*Sala, gaandu…*' I handed him over the cassette and yelled, 'Go see it for yourself. I am so ashamed to have a friend like you.' As he was getting on his car I couldn't help kicking him on the butt and yelling, 'I've stopped the spreading of this video all over the campus, but shouldn't have done so for a shameless bugger like you.' But he did not respond to that and drove off. That was the last time I saw Mote in the college.

I learnt shortly from other students that Mote had taken a transfer and joined some hotel management college elsewhere.

Mote's leaving the college did not sadden me in any way, and that was indeed strange considering the long association that I had with him.

ॐ

My relationship with Urmi predictably went beyond the platonic, though again, like any other love story, it all began with harmless visits to the South Lake – one of the nicer places in Calcutta with a large water body and clean places to sit and chat.

On the next sojourn there, I had expected Urmi to side with me when I had narrated her Mote's story and my parting ways with him. 'Good riddance,' I had said almost certain of her repeating the same in unison. But that did not happen, and she kept quiet for a while.

'Relationships are indeed enigmatic.' Urmi broke her silence as if she was talking to herself. She looked away from me and fixed her gaze on to a pack of swans paddling idly around the bank and said, 'Friendship is the hardest thing in the world to explain. It's not something you learn in school. But if you haven't learned the meaning of friendship, you really haven't learned anything.'

I looked at her in amazement as she replied, 'Not my quote, Muhammed Ali's'.

'Muhammed Ali? The greatest boxer on this planet ever?' I asked rather stupidly, wondering how a man who broke the noses of so many other people could have such deep understanding of friendship. Urmi nodded in affirmation and though I remained skeptical if the quote was actually Muhammed Ali's, I didn't spell it out.

'Oh!' I said, 'Friendship is unnecessary, like philosophy, like art.... It has no survival value,' but I too knew what I was saying was not from my heart.

That evening, the sweet nothings did not evoke the mushy feelings in either of us. I walked down after seeing off Urmi someplace near her home, wondering what was going on in her mind. It is impossible to read a girl's mind, but it occurred to me that she didn't quite approve of snapping any relationship.

However, next day I didn't broach upon the topic and Urmi was her usual boisterous self. She was a very interesting girl, not quite the same at all times. And that was not only with her attire which varied every day - jeans and top one day, *salwar* suit another. Not only her looks, but her behavior changed too – no not that she was happy one day, grumpy another. She was always cheerful. But some days she wanted to have a long walk, another day to go to the cinema, or on a rainy day just to soak in the rains in a secluded spot behind the college campus and indulge in frenzied kissing.

I learnt that *gol guppas, churmurs* and *achars* sold on the wayside attracted her as pollen would do to bees.

In fact, I was quite psyched to see her put in her mouth a dark piece of mango pickle that looked like soot fished out by the eczema-infected vendor with bare hands from a glass jar before putting them into a small paper bag that he picked up from the dirtiest corner of his cart.

My eyes had popped seeing her savour that with such pleasure as if she was having an orgasm.

'You wanna piece?' she queried.

'No, no, not at all.' I vehemently declined as I paid the vendor and moved away fearing that if Urmi purchased more of that unhealthy stuff, I would be forced to eat some of it.

On the way as I started lecturing her about the risks of putting into one's mouth whatever came on one's way. She chortled and said with a naughty wink, 'Putting into the mouth whatever comes in a girl's way…yeah can be unhygienic.' I didn't get her at first, but once I deciphered what she meant, it gave me goose bumps and an ineffable amorous feeling. Of course, till that time I hadn't graduated beyond kissing and petting.

But opportunity came my way to take the relationship deeper. Oh! That's rather a crude way to describe it. Oops, to put it literally… well before I do that let me tell you about my first drink. I had been advancing step by step from one sin to another.

One of the boys in the class had invited me to a party in a famous discotheque in Calcutta. He came from an affluent family, and there was no reason as to why he should be inviting me. But when he insisted that I come with Urmi, I understood why he did so. Urmi's presence would liven up any party.

I told Urmi about it, and she said, 'Yes, I too have been invited, and the guy insisted that I take you along.'

'Oh,' I couldn't hide my surprise.

'You'll be a great hit with the girls I suppose,' Urmi said in a teasing tone.

'Shall we go then?' I asked.

'Of course, who would miss a free entry to Bohemia?' she said.

'Bohemia is it?' I had little idea about discotheques, pubs and the five star hotels of Calcutta like any other guy coming from that stratum of the society which doesn't think beyond daily bread. The thought processes revolve only around how to make both ends meet today, tomorrow and day after.

'Yeah, great place.' Urmi said as if she was a regular there.

'You've been there?' I asked her casually, trying to gauge how the place was like, as I never had an experience of visiting such a place before.

'No, not yet,' Urmi confessed, but I know about it from my friends who are regulars there. I kept quiet, for I didn't quite rely on second hand information. But I learnt that almost all the girls in the class would be going. I was assured; I didn't want Urmi to be the only girl in a crowd of not-so decent boys. She would have been like a lamb amidst a pride of lions. I don't know why this comparison came to my mind, that I agree was rather primeval.

But as it turned out, it was indeed a great place. The ambience was electrifying and the party took off almost as soon as the doorman with a huge mustache and dressed in Rajasthani attire complete with turban and *nagra* shoes, ushered us in pushing the heavy wooden door.

We sat at a corner, and watched the girls and boys gyrating on the dance floor. A waiter went around with drinks. Urmi picked up a vodka cocktail and handed me over a Scotch with soda. I hesitated for a moment, for it was my first date with hard drinks. But I sipped a little and I found that it tasted quite good. I finished my glass and so did Urmi with hers. She then got up and dragged me to the floor. I was in a daze but danced to the tune of disco songs, the rhythm, the locale and Urmi's presence engulfed me like an inferno. It had set my senses on fire, and I started dancing like a madman. I drew Urmi close to me and dancing together I cannot recollect how long we were entwined in each other's arms as we lost track of time.

The party however got over too soon. At least we felt it that way and cursed the government (whosoever they were) for the Draconian law that forced all nightclubs and discotheques to close by midnight. But for the regulars, none were aware of this rule till the DJ belted out, 'This is the last number for the night, thereafter we've to close as per government rules.'

Ironically, he played, '*Raat baaki, baat baaki...*' before shutting down the music station.

Stepping out of the discotheque, as we were looking out for a taxi, one of the guys in our class offered us a lift in his car. He and his very sexy girlfriend (his tenth I supposed, and hers thirty-fifth or so as the college rumours went) sat in the front seats, and as soon as he pulled the car out of the curb she became extra cozy with him and it didn't require an astrologer to predict where she was putting her hands on to.

'How about coming to my place for a quickie dear?' he asked, and she agreed instantaneously. Thankfully, we were to be dropped before that, and luckily none of our parents were at home that night – my father had gotten a deputation to ISRO at Hyderabad and mother had followed him. Urmi's father had gone to the UK for some work, and her mother had gone along with him as well. Otherwise, we were in for some solid bashing from our parents for staying out so late in the night.

Sitting in the car with Urmi in the backseat, I remembered the guy driving the car lecture in the canteen sometime back, 'Whatever way even Salman Rushdie or Vikram Seth would have described it, sex is after all sex – messy, dirty and immensely pleasurable. Whatever preachers and poets may say about love, what really draws a guy to a girl is that forbidden union which Puritans may frown upon, but that's the reality guys – it's the excitement of running one's hand into … oh!' He had continued his discourse, much to the interest and liking of the boys. The way the girls giggled falling on each other seemed to me as if they too were enjoying what he said. But his final statement was indeed thought provoking, 'What else is there in a girl? Most of them don't know the difference between fine leg and extra cover, most of them would spend hours at the shopping mall unable to decide which top to buy…' he spelt out a long list of not so benign descriptions about girls, finally concluding, 'and above all, each one of them would treat her boyfriend as if he is a servant at her beck and call 24x7.' There was loud cheer from the crowd, though the girls had vehemently gestured thumbs down.

Urmi perhaps wasn't too different from the description of the girls that the guy had given in the canteen – she indeed had no idea of cricket field settings, she loved to shop and so on, but there was something extra in her that attracted me to her, as Mote had once said, 'like a magnet', besides because of the obvious sensation in certain part of my body while in her company.

I moved closer to Urmi in the backseat of the car. It was easier and more comfortable for us, without the gear stick in between, unlike the guy and the girl in the front seats.

Urmi however slapped hard on my hand when I tried to make a vulgar move. I cringed, and moved away from her. Thereafter, we looked outside in opposite directions and went to our respective homes from a midway spot where the guy dropped us. A wonderful evening culminating in that sort of a KLPD (Oh! I cannot expand the abbreviation, ask any college student from Delhi) was somewhat unexpected for sure.

But our parents not being at home for considerable time provided us with the opportunity to explore ourselves more closely. Not the right thing to do, we knew, but it just had to happen. And I discovered another of Urmi's trait that certainly was joyous.

Next day, Urmi was her present self, and only much later I came to know the reason behind her discordant behavior that evening was because of her period, and again a little afterward I learnt that during those days, all girls are subjected to tremendous mood swings.

A few days later it was Urmi's birthday, and a party with close friends at Peter Cat on Park Street was arranged by us. It was again a fabulous evening, and as we broke into singing, 'Happy Birthday to you…' I didn't know why but for a moment I felt that I missed Mote. But the thought came and went in a flash, as I got involved in the gaiety and merriment again.

'We'll have a bigger bash, next year,' I announced, little knowing that it was the last birthday that I would celebrate with Urmi in a very long time to come.

After the party, Urmi and I took a taxi back home. I kept safe distance from her, memories of the previous incident, not so long back being fresh in my mind. But strangely this time around she came closer, held me tightly and whispered into my ears, 'I am feeling like losing my virginity tonight.' I knew it could have been the effect of Smirnoff on her, but I too was quite under the influence of an inexplicable intoxication called love to have turned down the proposal and send her home.

So we landed at my empty house. She phoned the maid servant at home about her not returning that night and told her sternly, 'In case Ma, Baba call up tell them that I'm sleeping upstairs.'

'Is she reliable?' I queried. 'I mean she won't tell your parents that you go missing on some nights?' I added.

'She wasn't that reliable, till I saw her with the driver…err… in a compromising position, and assured her of keeping that secret a secret.' Urmi replied as a matter of fact.

'The driver doing it with the maid servant?' I gaped.

'Hmm,' Urmi chuckled wickedly, but did not elaborate. Neither was I interested in a love story involving a driver and maid servant.

That night was the night.

As usual it all started with the kisses, light ones on the cheeks, chins, lips that escalated into frenzied ones metamorphosing into licks, slurps and bites, yet retaining the charms of kisses. We were eager, we were tensed and for lack of any previous knowledge, I tried to replicate my act from some of the porn stuff that I had watched with Mote. But I was clumsy. So was Urmi. The clothes came off nevertheless, the *salwar kameez* and the shirt and trousers on the first go, the inners next, like unwrapping a chocolate bar first the paper wrapper, then the silver foil to expose the yummy kernel.

I looked at her unable to take my eyes off her. She was such a beautiful woman----tall, slender with smooth skin and inviting breasts. She reached for the light switch and the bright fluorescent tube made way to a dimmer night lamp. For a moment I couldn't see her, but in a while my eyes adjusted. She looked more inviting as the soft glow of the amber light spread all over her, creating an aura of ineffable mysticism. Then it happened. We sunk into the depths of an unfathomable ocean of pleasure and pain. After the pinnacle of an ineffable sensation that splashed like waves all over us, we lay naked entangled in each other's arms, exhausted and euphoric for a while that seemed to be eternity, yet I felt it was only fraction of a second that had passed in between.

'I didn't mean it to happen,' I said running my fingers into her hair, suddenly dawning on me that what we did was perhaps not right.

'Now that it has happened, you cannot make it un-happen again,' she chuckled and said, 'we'll make it happen again and again. I feel wonderful.'

'I love you,' I whispered.

'I love you too,' she whispered back.

'I shall never leave you,' I said.

'I shall not either, I promise,' she replied repeating slowly and embracing me tightly, 'I won't be able to live without you Anurag.'

In the days that followed – it was love and love all the way. There was nothing in my mind other than that. And I found, unlike what I had heard about girls; Urmi participated in the acts merrily, willingly and not like a dead fish, with me having to pester and pursue her into removing her clothes. She was naughty and she was adorable, and she was then into every tiny cell of my body, running through my veins, and inebriating my senses.

A few days later, I did not know from where, Urmi got a copy of a coffee-table illustrated Kama Sutra. She took it out from her bag in my house when we were all alone and said, 'Go through this book thoroughly, I don't want boredom to set in our relationship.' She spoke as if we were a couple for 25 years. Whatever it was, I liked the book and soon exhausted trying all the positions that were mentioned in that.

Being in love was wonderful, and not just physically. Things that we did together, like hanging around shops, going to music concerts or painting exhibitions brought about an inexplicable feeling of togetherness.

It was around these times that the famous Savage Garden song, 'Truly, Madly, Deeply,' was released and became a rage. It seemed to me as though the lyrics were penned for us.

I'll be your dream, I'll be your wish, I'll be your fantasy.
I'll be your hope; I'll be your love, be everything that you need.
I love you more with every breath, truly madly deeply do
I will be strong, I will be faithful 'cause I'm counting on a new
beginning.
A reason for living, a deeper meaning...

As we lay for long hours with her head on my chest listening to love songs I often wondered if heaven had descended on earth.

But life wasn't so beautiful forever. Soon, the world around me crumbled. I realised loving a girl was easy, shouldering the responsibilities weren't.

ℬ

It was like any other day, when I was sitting with Urmi in a secluded spot under a tree at the South Lake. My course had completed, and I was awaiting awarding of the degree. The dean's office had issued a provisional certificate to enable the students to apply for jobs. I had got that too, but was shot down in the two campus interviews that I had attended. I had printed at least 100 copies of my resume, and equal number of covering letters. Though many advised that writing the name of the company by hand on the top line, while the body of the letter was neatly typed created a bad impression I couldn't help it. I couldn't simply afford to get each and every covering letter typed individually, and though I had done for the first dozen or so letters, none of the companies even bothered to reply. I started talking about being hopeful of getting a job soon, though not sounding very convincing and held Urmi's hand. But she seemed to be 'off mood' that day and pulled her hand off. After a while I noticed that she hadn't uttered a word till then. That was indeed strange of her. 'Anything wrong?' I queried but instead of answering, she stunned me with the question, 'When are you marrying me?'

I was quite taken aback. Twenty two wasn't an age for anyone to get married. And besides, I didn't have a job either. For a modern girl like her, she shouldn't have even thought of marriage. A brilliant student she was, the thought of a career ahead would have come to her mind first. But there she was, behaving just like those *saree*-clad *puja-path walis* who have nothing other than marriage on their minds. They get married off at an early age to be servants in the house of the in-laws, cooking, cleaning, washing and raising children. I just could not place Urmi alongside with one of those images that flashed in my mind. But she repeated the line, this time slowly and firmly, 'I want you to marry me this month itself.'

'This month? Impossible.' I retorted. I shouted and repeated several times, 'impossible, impossible, impossible…'

Urmi kept quiet, and her eyes moistened. I tried to pacify her, the usual way any guy does in this type of situation.

'You know darling, as soon as I get a job, I will marry you. Besides, you have almost a year to go for your graduation. In case, your folks are pressing for marriage now, I will go myself and talk to them.' I said, and while saying so remembered that I had never met Urmi's parents till then.

Urmi got up abruptly, looking furious. I had never seen Urmi behaving like that before, and that had left me quite bewildered. 'Don't try to follow me, and don't call me darling ever,' she yelled at me and left hurriedly. I sat motionless, too confused even to think of what to do next. I sat below the tree for a long time, chewing strands of grass that I had uprooted unconsciously from the vicinity. My mind raced, but was unable to reach any destination.

Absentmindedly, I started throwing pebbles into the waters of the lake one after another. They sank without a trace. I hadn't noticed, but a young boy had been watching me. He came by my side, picked up a flat stone and threw it in a gliding fashion into the waters. The stone bounced several times on the water, went off to a considerable distance and then sank.

'There's a technique in everything,' an aged man, on all probability his grandfather commented from behind, 'If you are a stone, you'll sink anyway but if you hone yourself and there is someone to propel you with the right technique, you'll travel a little further.' After that prophetic statement, the aged man walked away from me with the little boy in tow. I sat there alone till darkness and mosquitoes forced me to leave the place.

As I walked down Southern Avenue, I lamented the fact that I was certainly like a stone and there was no one to guide me so as to make me traverse a little extra in life. I wondered what could have been the right technique in my situation. But thoughts of Urmi soon clouded those philosophical musings. I would surely marry Urmi, my life was incomplete without her. But how could I do that now? I had no job, and I knew that my parents would throw me out of their house, if I went there tugging along a newly wedded wife. Suddenly, I got very angry over Urmi – how could she be so inconsiderate?

I stood beneath a lamp post for a while, checking my watch. As I moved away from it, I noticed my shadow lengthen till it blended and vanished into the darkness of the footpath only to reappear at the next lamp post. I mulled foolishly, 'How much I try, the shadows keep following.' Suddenly, the shadows of gloom and despair seemed to be an intrinsic part of my being. I knew how much I tried, I couldn't shake them off.

As I came to the bus stop, I was overcome with a plethora of emotions – love, hate, anger, passion. I took a ticket to the bus stop nearest to Urmi's residence. I mustered all the courage, and walked straight into the white bungalow. There was no one to stop me at the cast iron gate that led to the building, and I walked up and stood right at the main entrance. I pressed the bell and waited beside the heavily sculptured mahogany wood door. An elegant lady, evidently Urmi's mother, opened it shortly. I would have preferred, if Urmi's parents were away, but more often than not things don't happen as per your wishes.

'Yes?' the lady queried in a surly tone.

I composed myself, pasted a 'door to door salesman' type of smile on my face and said, 'I'm Urmi's college mate. Is she at home?'

She frowned and replied, 'She has just come, but seems to be somewhat upset. I don't think she would like to see you now.' She said in a manner which was a clear hint that I should leave at once. But I was obstinate and demanded to see her over some 'very important college fest discussion'.

The sullen lady ushered me in rather reluctantly. I entered their very well decorated living room. A middle-aged handsome man, undoubtedly Urmi's father, was sitting on a sofa smoking a pipe and reading a file, as a large screen Sony TV beamed a news channel.

'*Namashkar* uncle,' I was as polite as I could be. The gentleman looked at me with a wince of disapproval on his face but pointed on to the sofa set gesturing me to sit. He did not speak to me but went on to reading that file as I looked around the room. Yes, they were certainly very rich and cultured. The sculptures, the pictures, the furniture everything oozed of class.

Urmi's mom had gone inside and came back with a glass of green sherbet. As she placed it on the coffee table in front of me, she said gruffly, 'If you are Anurag, Urmi doesn't want to see you.'

I don't know what took over me then, but I stood up in a flash and in the process, the corner of my bag that was hanging on to my right shoulder hit the sherbet glass and upturned it. The green fluid spread all over the red carpet, as the glass broke into pieces. I didn't care about that and began my speech of a lifetime.

'Look here, Sir and Madam. I love your daughter, and will marry her soon. At this point in time, I don't have a job and cannot do that right now. You shall have to bear with me for some time. But I promise I'll make your daughter very happy one day.' I paused for breath while mentally organising the next lines to say on how much I loved Urmi. But before I could utter another word, Urmi's father got up from his seat and slapped me hard across my left cheek.

'Get out of my house, you scoundrel,' he shouted at the top of his voice continuing, '*Tera aukat kya hai*? Don't even have a job and studying in that college of last benchers and have come to marry my daughter. What audacity? *Kaan kholke sun le*, Urmi is going to marry Deepak, and not you.' Like a typical Bengali in anger, he used a mix of Hindi and English to yell at me.

In spite of the pain and the insult, I muttered, 'Deepak, who?' I had never heard of him before.

'He is a brilliant, IIM graduate, and now an executive with Standard Chartered.' Urmi's mother replied with an air of boastfulness.

I again murmured, 'But does Urmi want to marry that Deepak?'

This time both Urmi's parents shrieked in unison, 'Of course, he is million times better than a vagabond like you.'

Then they both howled, 'Get out,' and Urmi's father almost pushed me out of the house. As I beat a hasty retreat, I heard Urmi's father yell, '*hey Bahadur, kaha ja ke marte hain, sab aire gaire ghus jaate hain andar.*' I knew he was addressing the *durban* of the house and it wasn't certainly flattering for any young man to hear his 'would be' father-in-law addressing him as '*aire gaire*', and treating him like a stray dog.

I left before Bahadur's entry into the room. There was no point in creating more scenes there. Besides, I was hurt and much wounded from inside. I strayed around Gariahat market for a while and then returned to my house. Thankfully, no one was there at home. I jumped on to my bed, buried my head into a pillow and sobbed.

∞

I desperately started looking for a job, any decent job would have done. But the very few interview calls that I received turned out to be lame ducks. I didn't know where from they got those questions. 'What is *Yakitori*?' I was asked in one interview when I told them that I was a foodie. They weren't happy with my answer that it was a Japanese dish (which I guessed from the name itself), and wanted more details. Much later I learnt that it was grilled chicken in Japanese. Then some one asked, 'Who was the swimmer who played the role of Tarzan?' when I had told them that I liked swimming. While I could answer Johnny Weissmuller correctly, I was stumped by the question as to how many Olympic gold medals he had won. In spite of being a good swimmer myself, I didn't have those statistics which I later learnt to be as five.

The questions were always followed by some sniping remark. In one of the interviews, I was so exasperated that when the smart alec interviewer of a company that were looking for insurance sales personnel asked me about the 'Save the Tiger' project, I retorted, 'True that the lives of tigers are at risk, but do you intend selling insurance policies to tigers as well?'. I was obviously shown the door in no time, but honestly I didn't feel that bad after seeing the annoyed face of the interviewer. He probably had never expected such a question from a jobless young man.

Insults and harassment became part of my life. That familiar sinking feeling that made my limbs numb and senses dumb recurred again and again. I felt totally lost and it appeared to me that I was sucked into a never-ending whirlpool of bad luck and melancholia. A sense of inferiority complex seeped into my psyche that deflated my confidence like a pin prick into a balloon.

But I got lucky one day. There was an interview call from Pan India Airlines who were looking to recruit flight pursers. I wasn't at all hopeful of getting this job, and thought of dropping it. But then my parents were at home, and just in order to avoid them for some time, I chose to attend the interview. As I was getting dressed, mom asked, 'Going to a party or what?'

'No, interview.' I replied, combing my hair.

'Where?' She asked.

'Pan India Airlines,' I answered. Father had by then entered the room, and made a scornful remark, 'Pan India Airlines will close down if they recruit a duffer like you.' Mom agreed with him and added a few more contemptuous lines. I thought, 'What a great start to the day!' as I left the house many hours before the interview, just to avoid them.

On my way to the interview, a cat crossed my path, I was forced to walk below a ladder that was put up to paint a building, and then I saw a single *shalik* bird, which were all signs of bad luck.

I walked down to the tram terminus and boarded a tram. A tram ride could be fun, if one was not in a hurry. And I was not. Boarding a tram from the terminus had an added advantage that one could choose his own seat. I boarded the first class coach. Though the tickets were costlier by 50 paise, it was worth it. Two huge fans cooled the cabin and the left side window seats were all singles. I sat on the front most one just behind the driver's cabin. The tram set off its journey with just about a dozen passengers on board the first class coach and with the usual clanks, clatters and tings.

Seated on the wooden seat, watching the standing driver shift the impedance lever in a semi-circular arc from left to right, right to left to increase or decrease speed, I wondered what it took to be a tram driver. He tapped a button with his right foot often that emitted the unique 'tram bell' ring with its characteristic tings. There was no need to ring it often, but perhaps trams made every effort to make their presence felt, after several groups lobbied for their removal from the city. There were arguments and counter-arguments.

> '*Trams are slow.*'
> '*Not everyone is in a hurry*'.
> '*Trams lead to traffic jams.*'
> '*They don't pollute the atmosphere.*'
> '*Tram, tram go away.*'
> "*Tram, tram, the elders' pram.*'

But trams had an exclusivity associated with them. They shared the road with the pedestrians, the yellow taxis, the snazzy Suzukis and the Toyotas, the hand-pulled rickshaws, obeyed the traffic signals, and yet followed their own predetermined ways, one behind another. They could not overtake; neither could they speed up at will. I remembered a tête-à-tête that took place between my father and a friend of his who worked as a clerk in a government office and always took the tram to work. Those were during my school days, when my parents were a lot relaxed, and when the 'ghost' of their son's career thoughts hadn't insinuated into their souls.

My father had asked in jest, 'Ramratanbabu, why is it that you always take the tram, when there are faster modes of transport like minibuses to go to Dalhousie Square?'

Ramratanbabu, displaying his typical laid back attitude, had then blown into the steaming tea cup, which I had noticed he did out of habit and even if the tea was cold. He had then dipped a 'Thin Arrowroot' biscuit into it and only after relishing the succulence of the soft biscuit and a sip of tea he spoke as I tried to figure out why the biscuit manufacturer bragged so much about the crunchiness of their biscuits when most Bengalis dipped them into tea before eating them.

Ramratanbabu had replied with a sigh, 'I love trams.' He paused and repeated the earlier process of savoring his tea-biscuit as I watched the biscuit wane from full to half, to one fourth and then vanish entirely into his mouth. The teacup was still half full from my point of view, half empty from his (maybe) when he elaborated further on the similarity between trams and his life.

'They resemble my life. Slow and lack of ambitions.' He started to pause almost immediately like a tram facing an obstacle just after starting. The tea-biscuit ritual followed. Only after his second cup of tea and fourth biscuit he added pace to his confessions and comparisons. 'Trams resemble my life, they have to trail the one ahead. I will never get a promotion ahead of my seniors. Government rules you know.'

Father had nodded his head in agreement.

'Trams resemble my life. They have no steering. They have to just follow where life takes them.'

'Life or line?' Ramratanbabu had ignored my mother's taunt.

'Trams resemble my life. In spite of being the grandest of the road, they are left far behind. Trams resemble my life. They have to obey every traffic signal as I have to--- from the boss, to wife and children. Trams resemble my life. They are slow, silent like any aged person and the younger generation wants them out.' Ramratanbabu had ended his rhetoric with another sigh and moist eyes.

So far so on the philosophies and similes, but in a quirky twist of fate, he had died succumbing to injuries that he had suffered when he fell alighting a tram. I don't know if he had muttered then, 'Trams resemble my life. You are always hurt by those whom you love.'

I came back to the present having startled by the conductor tapping on my shoulder for the fare. I reached for my purse in my hip pocket, but could not find it. I got up, tried to feel if it had sunk deeper inside, but could not locate it. 'Seems that I have lost my purse,' I gave an apologetic and folly-laced smile that had become a natural part of my persona. The conductor tightened his grip on my shoulders, 'Ha, another act not to pay the fare I suppose.' He raised his gruff voice that drew attention of the passengers around.

Unsolicited comments flew in then one by one:-

'The youth these days would do anything to cheat the government.'

'There is no hope for the country.'

'If not the country, the tram company for sure.'

'The boy should be handed over to the police.'

'Ha, police. They would treat him to some snacks. The police in our country are always pals to the crooks.'

'Yes, snacks for the petty criminals, dinner for the bigger fishes, that's our police.'

A rumbling laughter swept the tram in unison.

'May be the boy's pocket was picked, after all he doesn't look like a criminal'. There was an interruption from a female voice from one of the ladies seat behind and mercifully she spoke against the motion.

I turned my head but couldn't spot the woman who had spoken. But there were some voices in support of her. 'And in a way he is right not to pay the fare. This is a filthy tram anyway with broken seats and the fan blades moving like the hour hand of a clock.'

'Hour hand was surely an exaggeration,' I thought, 'Minute hand should have been more apt.' But there was sudden change in stance and all the passengers started agreeing that the ride wasn't worth paying for. The conductor loosened his grip considering that public opinion was turning against the company for whom he collected the fare. I then remembered that there could be a two rupee coin in one of the pockets of my rucksack. After a little bit of struggle, thankfully I could fish it out. I handed it over to the conductor with a smile of an athlete on the Olympic victory stand.

I flopped down on the seat that I owned legitimately after paying one rupee and fifty paise. The conductor had returned a glossy fifty paise coin, which I carelessly shoved into my rucksack. Esplanade was still some distance away and I had now the opportunity and leisure to look out of the huge open window of the tram. The tram went past a huge hospital. 'I could have tried to become a doctor,' I mused. No one had ever heard of unemployed doctors. I discarded the thought instantaneously, for I knew I could have never become a doctor. It was a profession meant for super-brilliant students.

A little later, when the tram had moved on, leaving the hospital behind and I could see the black fairy atop the magnificent Victoria Memorial, I tried to organise my thoughts. Certainly my pocket was picked and I lost my companion of many years, a faded purse, shredded at the corners. In a flash I remembered there was nothing much inside. I smiled as the thief's handiwork would have enriched him with a torn purse, a few useless papers and just a ten rupee note. 'How to go back home without any money?' was a poser that I decided to worry about later on. I looked up at the fairy again. She was supposed to rotate in accordance with the direction of the wind but was motionless. 'She must be a sad fairy', I concluded.

As I reached Pan India Airlines office on Chittaranjan Avenue, I saw a lady getting out of a white Ambassador car in front of it. But just at this point in time, a seedy looking man came running from an adjacent lane, snatched off her handbag and fled. Instinctively, I ran after the man, outpaced him in no time and got hold of his collar. I seized the bag as a crowd that had gathered instantaneously started showering slaps on him. I went to the lady and said, 'Here's your bag, Ma'am.' The matronly lady, who feebly took it back, was visibly very upset. True, no one could have imagined such a theft in broad daylight at the central business district of Calcutta.

'Thank you son,' she said, adding, 'there were some important documents inside.' She left escorted by a number of security personnel who had then come out of the Pan India Airlines building.

The initial part of the interview went on as usual, the registration, the fairly long wait in the lounge for my turn and so on. Then as I entered the interview room to face a three-member panel, I was in for a pleasant surprise.

The elderly lady whose bag was stolen was among the panelists for the interview. She introduced herself, 'I am Mrs. Deepa Malhotra,' and I am the chairman of this Board. She then introduced me to the two men who flanked her, one of whom looked like a thug and another like a pig. 'Mr. Chandu,' she pointed out to the guy one on her left who looked at me with an expressionless face. 'Mr. Saini,' she pointed out to the man who kept munching on to some cashew nuts from a plate kept in front of him. He tried to act smart and said, 'Madam you're the chairperson, and not chairman.' He laughed at his own remark but Mrs. Malhotra ignored him totally and I felt she had deliberately said so to show who the 'man' in the interview board was. She made no attempt to disclose that she had met me before and I too behaved like a perfect stranger.

The two men tried to heckle me and began firing some questions, but Mrs. Malhotra cut them short and asked me to tell them something about myself. I put in my best in replying and after listening to me for a while, she commented, 'Yes, we need such bright young people for our airline,' and signaled the end of the interview, leaving the other two men quite baffled. But they kept quiet, for they couldn't probably question the decision of the chairperson of the Board.

Coming out of the building I wondered if I would really make it, for a flight purser's job seemed to be a dream at that point of time. The pay was good and I would get an opportunity to see many places. 'Leaving Urmi behind after marriage for long flights however would be very painful.' I was weaving dreams as I walked down to the Esplanade metro station. I had borrowed some money from a friend who too had come for the interview. He had gladly lent the money learning that my pocket was picked and I was totally broke. On the train however, I became more pragmatic and thought, 'How silly of me, thinking of marrying Urmi after that fiasco, and when there is no sight of a job as yet.'

I had nothing to do in the next few days. There were no job interviews, and there was no Urmi either to give me company in my loneliness. I spent long hours in the cybercafés which had come up in every nook and corner of the city, surfing the only Indian job site that existed at that time---naukri.com, and applied for every job opening that looked for freshers. Most of the times, I did that, rest of the time I surfed porn sites furtively, like any other normal guy of my age.

I did not try to get in touch with Urmi, for I wanted to first get a job and go back to her with an engagement ring, one which I had seen in the showcase of P.C.Chandra Jewellers' showroom. 'I will marry her as soon as I got a job,' I thought. Her parents despised me, but she had wanted to marry me and that was what only mattered in accordance with the old adage that said the *kaazi* had no say, if the *mia* and *bibi* were willing.

But, there was disappointment in store for me. A few days later, I received a marriage invitation card by post, sent by one of my friends in college that proclaimed the marriage of Urmi with Deepak. It said, in the usual format,

Brigadier (Retd.) Dhanraj Banerjee, Director- Rishra Alloy Company and Mrs. Rupa Banerjee, M.A, Chairperson- Friends of Crows of Calcutta, NGO, cordially invites you on the auspicious

occasion of the marriage of their only child Urmi with Deepak,
*M.B.A (**IIM**, Calcutta), Financial Executive, **Standard Chartered***
on... I paused to wonder if the words IIM and Standard
Chartered were highlighted in bold only to make a mockery of
my status.

I read on to learn that the marriage ceremony was taking
place in just ten days' time and the reception was arranged in
the banquet hall of Hotel Hyatt Regency. I paced up and down,
clenching my fist, that feeling of helplessness and sorrow engulfing
all my senses. I felt like crying once again, but fought with my
emotions to hold back my tears. And though I knew that Urmi's
father was a retired army man, I didn't know that her mother too
was a biggie as well. 'But what is this NGO about – do they keep
a count of crows in Calcutta skies or protect them?' I wondered
without being able to make heads or tails out of it and said to
myself, 'Why do they have to print their resume on a marriage
invitation card?' I tore the card into many pieces and threw them
out of the window.

'Why does Urmi have to get married in such a hurry?' I thought
over it again and again. She knew very well that I was not in a
position to marry her then, and she had put up an act to get rid of
any guilt associated with the relationship that we had. She could
always console herself, 'Well, I had asked him for marriage first.
He only had refused.' I was certain that it was all stage managed.
She really wanted to marry an established person, who would
be respected in society and not someone who was likely to end
up being a clerk in a courier company or waiter in a restaurant.
I was just a time-pass for her. If she had really loved me, she
certainly could have waited for some time till I stood on my
own feet.

৪০

However, something almost like a miracle happened a few days later. I got an envelope from Pan India Airlines, confirming my employment as a flight purser. I had a job; finally. I took the envelope in my hand and rushed to Urmi's house. It was already evening when I reached there. It was bedecked with strings of blue colored tiny light-bulbs, and looked mesmerizing from a distance. I rushed inside pushing the iron gate open, when the watchman confronted me. 'Urmi,' I uttered only a word panting.

'*Oh, aap shaadi ki liye aye hain?*' he asked me innocently.

'Yes,' I nodded in agreement, not wanting to waste any time over arguments.

'*Lekin who log to sab Hyatt gaya hain,*' he informed me. I ran back to the bus-stand remembering that it had skipped my mind that it was the day of Urmi's marriage. I reached Hotel Hyatt Regency shortly afterwards and went straight inside. In spite of the 'Rights of Admission Reserved' board on the outside, and I, in spite of not being an invitee or customer or guest, the watchmen at the gate let me inside without any questioning. It wasn't difficult to locate the banquet hall with a board outside declaring, 'Urmi weds Deepak.' I pushed the heavy door of the banquet hall and entered. It was very crowded inside. I spotted Urmi sitting on a throne-like chair in her red bridal attire at a far corner. There was a small queue of invitees in front of her handing over their gifts one by one. I pushed my way through the crowd and went right in front of her.

'Urmi,' I called out her name and shouted waving the Pan India Airlines appointment letter envelope in my right hand, 'I have got a job, and you have to marry me.' Then, a hall full of people turned their attention towards me. I yelled again, 'I have got a job Urmi, a good job as a flight purser in Pan India Airlines.'

A violent looking man in bridegroom's attire came over to me and punched me in my face, 'Get out immediately. Urmi is now my wife. Ha, a flight purser's job – go remove dirty trays or clean the passengers' vomit.'

Urmi stood up and came close. She repeated in the same lines, 'Get out now, as he says. Ha, how could you think that I would marry a waiter on an airplane?'

I tried to reason, 'Urmi, no job is ignoble, Gandhiji had said,' not quite sure if at all Gandhiji said so. But then, wasn't he the person who said most of the good things that Indians generally quote? I tried to augment my argument with more comparisons, 'And why even Sanjeev Kapoor is only a chef, but he is loved and respected by all. Not only that, he is stinking rich as well. And think of Javed Habib, he is only a barber…' But I couldn't finish my sentences, for they had called in the security, and four tough men lifted me up and took me out of the banquet hall, as I screamed, 'Urmi-eeeeeeeeeeeeee, I looooooooooooooooove you.'

The four security men were comparatively more sensible. They took me to some room in an annex-building, gave me a soft drink and advised, 'Now go home, and don't watch too many Shah Rukh Khan movies.' I staggered out of the swanky hotel with many happy people inside. In spite of giving me the job, I cursed Pan India Airlines. I knew that they were notorious for delays, but this delay in giving me the job had cost me my love. And this time around they wouldn't be apologising either, '*is deri ke liye khed hain.*'

I wandered aimlessly on the streets of Calcutta and came somewhere near Chitpore. I heard someone whisper in my ears, '*Saab*, drinks and girls close by.' He spoke as if he was appointed by the government with the job of dispelling my sorrow like a true friend. I turned around to look at him, expecting to see a squalid unshaven man in tattered clothes whom I had to shoo away. But the man I confronted was in old clothes no doubt, but they were clean, and he had bright eyes and trimmed beard. It occurred to me that I had seen this middle-aged man somewhere, but could not recall immediately. I was somewhat hypnotised by the way he spoke and followed him. He guided me through a maze of alleys, lanes and by-lanes and stopped in front of an old big building. He tapped on a heavy wooden door thrice and I was greeted with the beats of music that seeped out from inside as the door parted open. A very old gatekeeper gazed at me with piercing eyes and taking charge from the other man, escorted me to a small room. I was made to wait for a short while on a clean bed which was the only furniture there. A plump lady, in her fifties came in, smiled sweetly and sat down beside me. 'What do you want *Saab*?' She asked me in a melodious voice. I wondered what to say, and it then struck me that what I did driven by loneliness and sorrow wasn't proper. I was right inside a brothel and there was no escape route.

Strangely, however, the pimp and the *mausi* never appeared to be disgusting. They had an aura of elegance around them. I picked out my purse from my trouser back pocket and checked. There was not much of money left. I pleaded helplessness and said, 'I don't have much money' and handed over the purse to her. She didn't touch it, but asked, 'How much?' I counted and confessed, 'A little more than two hundred rupees.' 'How much can you spare? After all you may have something important to buy, may be medicines on your way back, besides the bus fare.' She asked me and I was overwhelmed by her consideration. 'About this much, leaving out the bus fare,' I replied as if opiated while handing her the two hundred rupee notes. 'That won't buy you a drink and all you can get for this amount is to watch a strip show. Come again later with at least five hundred rupees for a more wholesome treat,' she said with a sigh and then a wink. She directed me to follow her and led to a larger room where I sat down on a carpet with a bunch of drunken strangers. They seemed to be eagerly waiting for an event to start. Soon a *qawali* started playing over two speakers which I noticed were fixed near the ceiling of the wall. The fluorescent lights went off and a blue glow filled the room. A girl came in through a curtained door on the other side, and instantly there was commotion amongst the spectators who greeted her with low whistles. The lights came on dimly and I could see the girl draped in a bright red *salwar* suit with golden embroidery all over. She stamped on the floor, as the *ghungrus* on her legs came to life. The *ghungrus*, a dancing accessory made of a collection of tiny bells tied to a strip of leather and strapped on both shins was introduced by the Mughals and formed an indispensable part of any Indian dance form, a fact that I had once learnt from Urmi who had keen interest in classical dances.

There was a loud cheer as the young girl started gyrating with the crescendo of the song's tempo. The psychedelic lights were switched on adding to the dramatic effect of the show. It went on for a while, when another girl joined her. I looked at their faces, beautiful, tired and distant. Songs changed from *qawalis* to *gazals* to popular Hindi numbers and just as the crowd was getting restless, off came the *ghungrus* from the ankles. There was some more music and some more songs, when the girls seductively removed their tops. Then after a few more songs, the girls were dancing wearing only black and white frilled bras and the *pyjamas*. The next predictable move on their part was to remove the *pyjamas* and they started dancing wearing just bras and panties, both with decorative laces. This went on for a while as a boy started serving liquor in small glasses. He collected money from the patrons handing over a glass to each of them and when he came close to me, I gestured a 'not required' sign with my palm. But the boy handed me over a glass and said, 'Complimentary from madam, for first time visitors.' I sipped the cheap liquor that was pretty strong. A while later, my head clouded, but my senses sharpened amidst a huge uproar from the spectators as the girls removed their tops. The girls were young, fair and their breasts firm, yet it wasn't a pretty sight. There was a little more, when they stripped fully. The crowd lapped the hapless girls from their heads to toes with lewd popping eyes. I was however depraved of any amorous feeling that any man would feel ogling at naked young girls. The agony and misery that these girls had to undergo by selling their dignity and their bodies were evident and far from enticing.

The music stopped abruptly, the girls picked up the clothing from the floor and ran off inside. A grunt of disappointment swept across the room, as the boy who served liquor declared that the show was over. I felt relieved. We were led out through a long corridor lined with small rooms where women in garish make-ups huddled together, struck lascivious poses and made catcalls to the passing men. Some stopped for a quick bargain and a quicker relief from their pent up passion. I staggered out into the open air; the liquor by then had made inroads into the veins to make me anesthetised of any grief that were an integral part of my being those days. I looked around, trying to figure out in which direction to go, when the pimp who had brought me there came close to me. He said, '*Saab*, you may not be able to find your way back. I will take you to the nearest bus stop. He seemed to have a swig and was in an elated mood as he crooned, '*Yeh dunia, yeh mehfil mere kaam ki nahin…*' 'This world, this revelry is not for me…' I heard his soulful voice, and then it struck me where I had seen him. He was a theatre personality from yesteryears. He accompanied me to the nearest bus stop and vanished into the darkness still humming the evergreen Mohammed Rafi song, without bidding me goodbye. I waited for a bus, the rhythmic *'chham chhams'* of the *ghungrus* still ringing in my ears reverberating pain and poverty. I then recollected that the plump lady whom I had seen in the brothel was a famous cabaret artist who was featured in some movies as well. I felt miserable and squatted to puke into an iron mesh of a drain. 'Life is indeed strange,' I thought as I hauled myself up to hail a taxi, 'you never know where it will take you.' Life, not the taxi of course; for the latter duly dropped me in front of my house.

Unfortunately I returned home when my parents had come back. They could smell liquor in my breath. Mother seemed stunned and father mumbled something about 'being a disgrace to the family' and slapped me hard. Too many blows on a single day; I passed out only to wake up the next morning.

*****

4

ZINDAGI KI SAFAR, HAIN YEH KAISA SAFAR...

Next day, it was my birthday, but my parents left for some unknown place after telling me to get lost for the day repeating the same line as to how ashamed they were to have me as their son. Thankfully, Mom had given me breakfast and I ate as much as I could figuring out that it might not be till night when I could get my next meal. That again incited them to slander me comparing my eating to that of a pig's, a favourite phrase of theirs. I was angry and, though at one point in time I thought of throwing the plate away and leaving the dining table but restrained myself. After all I was then quite used to insults and abuses from all quarters.

When I hit the streets, I didn't know where to go. I kept walking aimlessly. As I was walking past the Ramakrishna Mission's imposing building, a placard caught my eye. It displayed in bold letters, 'Teachings of Swami Vivekananda... a discussion by eminent scholars.' It further said that entry to the event was free. I checked my watch. The event was to begin in another ten minutes. I hesitated for a while, but then decided to go inside. It would be at least better to remain inside an air-conditioned hall for some time than to roam around the streets of Calcutta in the scorching sun.

I had gone into the lecture hall only to kill time, and escape the weather outside, but that free discourse and discussion on Swami Vivekananda completely changed my view towards life. It was perhaps God's decision that I chanced to go there, and that too on my birthday. When I came out of the hall, I had turned into a new person.

Like any Bengali, I had heard of Swami Vivekananda, but knew nothing about him. I chose a seat in the back of the near-empty hall planning to fall asleep, when a fair, handsome *sanyasi* in saffron robe called out to me, 'Son, why don't you come forward.' His command was impossible to ignore and I reluctantly took a seat near the dais, wherefrom I had no option but to intently listen to all that was spoken.

'For those who don't know anything about Swami Vivekananda, let me introduce him to you,' said the first speaker.

He was an excellent orator, and I was enthralled while listening to him. I came to know many unknown facts about Swamiji. He was born on 12th January 1863 as Narendra Nath Datta in a traditional Bengali family. His father, Vishwanath Datta, was an attorney in Calcutta High Court and his mother Bhuvaneswari Devi was a pious lady, who called her son Vireshwar, after Lord Shiva. His mother had deep influence on him and later in his life, he often quoted her favorite line, 'Remain pure all your life; guard your own honour and never transgress the honour of others. Be very tranquil, but when necessary, harden your heart.' I memorised the line, for it would be my mantra in life too.

Narendra (as Swamiji was called then) had deep interest in varied subjects from philosophy to religion, mathematics to sciences. He was an avid sportsman too and took part in a number of games. Even when he was young, he questioned the validity of superstitious customs and discrimination based on caste and refused to accept anything without rational proof.

The next speaker in a long flowing robe talked at length about Swamiji's life beyond his childhood. I was fascinated by what he said about Swamiji and became his follower instantly. He read out a number of Swamiji's quotes, some of which that got embedded in my mind are as follows:

"It is our own mental attitude which makes the world what it is for us. Our thoughts make things beautiful, our thoughts make things ugly. The whole world is in our minds. Learn to see things in the proper light. First, believe in this worl."

"Face the brutes. That is a lesson for all life—face the terrible, face it boldly.'

"The earth is enjoyed by heroes—this is the unfailing truth. Be a hero. Always say, 'I have no fear.'"

"After every happiness comes misery; they may be far apart or near. The more advanced the soul, the more quickly does one follow the other. What we want is neither happiness nor misery. Both make us forget our true nature; both are chains--one iron, one gold; behind both is the Atman, who knows neither happiness nor misery. These are states, and states must ever change; but the nature of the Atman is bliss, peace, unchanging."

"Knowledge can only be got in one way, the way of experience; there is no other way to know."

"No one should be judged by their defects. The virtues a person has are his especially; his errors are the common weaknesses of humanity and should never be counted in estimating his character."

There were many such quotes, and I was spellbound listening to them. I was transformed into another world, hitherto unknown to me. When the lectures got over, I came out feeling stronger to fight this big, bad world. I purchased a book of Swamiji's quotes and a tiny laminated picture of Swamiji from a counter outside which were to be part of my belongings that I would always carry thereafter. They were to be a source of inspiration during times of distress, a source of solace during times of sorrow. And many years later, when life took me through its twists and turns, I never parted with these.

In a way I was reborn on my 23ʳᵈ birthday.

৪৩

'I have been posted in Delhi,' I told my parents, not disclosing that I had specifically opted for a posting at any place other than Calcutta. Father did not lift his face from *The Telegraph*, and just let out an expressionless, 'hmm.' Mom commented, 'we must thank God for his job; at least we won't have to feed him throughout our lives.'

Mom and Dad were obviously unhappy, they knew all I would be doing was to serve food to the passengers and do the work of a waiter in the air, however attractive my uniform might be. They could never say, 'My son is a flight purser,' with that air of pride which other parents could, 'My son is a doctor, my son is an engineer, my son is an IAS officer, my son is a chartered accountant... and so on.' It was outside the ambit of professions that are classified as 'noble' in our society.

'No job is ignoble,' I tried to convince them, 'Rajinikanth started his career as a bus conductor.' I tried to think of other great men who had humble beginnings, but father cut me short.

'Ha, now he will talk about Bill Gates and Dhirubhai Ambani who never went to college,' father commented with the newspaper still covering his face. Mom agreed with him and let out a sneering chuckle.

Strangely though, a few days later, as I was leaving for Delhi, they insisted on accompanying me to the airport. At the airport as I was to enter the departure lounge, even more surprisingly, mom hugged me tight, planted a kiss on my forehead and said in a tearful voice, 'Take care of yourself, son.' I could have been mistaken, but I saw my father's eyes moisten when I got up from touching his feet, the act of *pranam* coming to me almost instinctively. He had earlier given me an envelope full of cash, and an add-on credit card as well, the actions not quite in sync with the persona that I had known for so many years.

I put up in an ordinary lodge in Karol Bagh. A friendly clerk at Pan India Airlines' Calcutta office had given the phone number and address of this lodge, after knowing that I had no place to stay in Delhi. 'When our staff goes to Delhi, they stay in this lodge, which gives Pan India Airlines employees good discount,' he had informed. I was accommodated in a room constructed quite evidently illegally on the roof. The very friendly receptionist, who was extremely courteous in spite of looking like a gangster, told me, 'Stay as long as you like, but you shall have to make seven days payment in advance.' However, I did not have to stay there for long, as I moved into a well-furnished servant-quarter of a senior manager of Pan India Airlines in Vasant Vihar along with another trainee flight purser. I learnt that letting out the servant quarter, after furnishing it was against the rules of the company, but in Pan India Airlines, company rules were applicable only to the common employees and not the high and mighty. No one dared to say anything about them, for fear of a transfer or getting dropped in the next promotion. But it suited me fine, for it was impossible to get a cheaper accommodation in Delhi, particularly in a place like Vasant Vihar.

I did not like my room-mate, but I had no choice. All the other guys had some accommodation as a majority of them were from Delhi. The day my room-mate brought in his girlfriend for a screw, he just ordered me out, 'Bro, you gotta get lost this evening, and come back only after ten in the night.' So, I had no other option than to hang around in the Priya cinema complex for several hours doing nothing. I tried to get a ticket for any movie, but there were 'House Full' signs against every movie name on the display board. To add insult to injury, he offered me one fourth of a pizza that had gone cold after I entered the room at the time he had specified. I declined the offer, for I had already filled myself with *chana-bhatora*, a delectable Punjabi dish of chickpeas curry and Indian fried flatbread from a roadside stall. Of course even if I hadn't, I wouldn't have eaten that leftover of his. He of course chomped off the remains of the pizza and threw the box at one corner of the room. I presumed he had a good fuck, or rather several good fucks going by the contented look on his face, and a number of empty condom sachets strewn around. Thankfully, he had disposed off the used condoms by flushing them off in the commode. The last stubborn one, a portion of which was still popping out of the commode outlet was flushed off by me, when I noticed it with utter disgust.

But I started loving the job and Pan India Airlines. Contrary to what people thought about flight pursers, I found out that it was an excellent profession. It was a very highly skilled job, and one had to keep the numerous safety aspects in mind. Serving the passengers gave one a sense of satisfaction, something akin to the feeling of those who serve the nation, like doctors, nurses, farmers, soldiers and so on.

The initial training program that I had to attend in a classroom carved out of a decommissioned airplane, parked outside the training school, was interesting. The instructor with a French beard, who appropriately utilised every opportunity to touch the girls at inappropriate places while teaching them how to wear life jackets, was otherwise a nice man. He talked at length on how important we were for the airline and that our primary job was to ensure safety to the passengers. 'You are ambassadors of the airline, an airline is recognised by its cabin crew,' he kept repeating this line which we all loved. Later on I learnt that he was a flight purser at one time, but was grounded on the complaints of a safety officer, who had caught him kissing an airhostess behind the curtains of the rear galley, as the aircraft was landing into Bombay. 'This is the nature of many people in our country. They cannot accept the fact that someone else is enjoying life more than them,' the guy who told me about the instructor had concluded with that line. I, of course, didn't find the safety officer's act an outcome of jealousy – a flight purser involved in such activities that could have indeed jeopardised the safety of the aircraft definitely needed to be punished.

Another lady, an airhostess who had opted for a ground job due to some medical condition, took other classes. She trained us on how to serve food and liquor to the passengers, how to deal with a drunken passenger, how to clear the mess when someone had puked and so on. I sighed; the job had its hazards as well. But I remembered what Swamiji had said, "Those who serve mankind, are actually serving God," and so any humiliating thoughts when I was to pick up dirty trays with half eaten food did not cross my mind.

The classroom training went on for a couple of months, after which we were put on board operating aircraft flying to different destinations.

I started enjoying myself after a long time since my breakup with Urmi. For the first time in my life, I got to stay in five-star hotels, and that was something which I could have never afforded on my own, whatever job with my qualifications I did. Adding to the job-satisfaction was the fat pay and the chance to see so many places. The company took care of almost everything, providing transportation, food, uniform and even allowances for washing them while on duty.

I, however, could not pick up a girl. I liked one, who was cute and had joined the airline recently, but she made it amply clear that she would date only pilots. True, the pilots in any airline were the biggies – respected and awed by one and all. And they made a lot of money. It was the natural choice for all unmarried airhostesses to try and latch on to pilots.

I led a bachelor's life, watching movies on my own, or drinking coffee all alone in Café Coffee Day outlets or eating ice-cream from Nirula's. My roommate fortunately then had different work hours, and so I didn't have to kill time outside when he screwed his girlfriend.

I was getting absorbed in the job; interacting with so many different people every day made life really fascinating. Many celebrities boarded the flights, and it was a joy to see them from close. I was star-struck watching Shah Rukh Khan and Anil Kapoor, who were avid readers and spent most of the time reading magazines on board. I marveled at Malaika Arora and Bipasha Basu's stunning figures, Hema Malini and Sridevi's grandeur, Kajol's childlike ways and so on. The celebrities had something in them that made them to stand out from the *aam junta*. I was amused to see that while disembarking at Bombay airport, much to the delight of everyone on board, Siva Mani, the famed percussionist played a few beats with the drum that he was carrying. He made the day for the deplaning passengers who thoroughly enjoyed his act.

Then, one day I saw Sachin Tendulkar, Saurav Ganguly, Rahul Dravid and the entire Indian cricket team from close. It was indeed a memorable flight. But there was a little embarrassment in store for me, when I exclaimed involuntarily, 'Arre Kapil Dev,' on suddenly coming face to face with him. I just could not control myself seeing my childhood hero in flesh and bones. And what a towering personality he possessed! Thankfully, the great man just nodded, smiled at me and got down without taking offence.

There were many men and women at the pinnacle of fame and glory who boarded the planes every now and then and I watched them from close with awe and reverence. In a way it was a bonus, not many professions gave one such an opportunity.

ꝏ

A few months only into the job, but I thought I had learnt the tricks of the trade fairly well. It was my first international flight and we were landing into Bangkok. I, seeing the other cabin crew, had shoved in a few miniature liquor bottles meant for the passengers into my bag. It was more or less the norm – serve the passengers a little less (well for their good and the crew's good as well, for who wanted a drunken brawl at 35,000 feet above the ground?) and pilfer a few for your consumption. Mr. Gupte, the senior flight purser with a big moustache had caught me in the act and asked sternly, 'Hey what are you doing?'

I was naturally taken aback and mumbled, 'Err.. I mean everyone is taking. I am sorry Sir.' I prepared to take out the bottles that I had taken.

'No, you need not take them out, but next time be careful,' he said, explaining further, 'When you take things from the aircraft, put them in a separate bag. In case you are caught, just say that it isn't your bag.'

I heaved a sigh of relief as he showed me the goodies, miniatures of Johnny Walker Black Label, packets of cashew nuts, juices, coffee sachets and the like packed in a duffle bag which he had brought specifically for the theft. No one really seemed to mind lifting things from the aircraft; they were taken like perks that came with the job.

In Bangkok, Mr. Gupte gave me some job related valuable advice like how to deal with ministers and VIPs when they travelled aboard Pan India Airlines before promising to take me to the most eye-popping show that I had ever seen. After drowning the first stolen Scotch whisky of my life, sitting in a five-star hotel room in Bangkok, I said in tipsy voice, 'I am sooooo lucky that I got this job.'

'Lucky, ha?' Mr. Gupte went into a pensive mood, and said in a prophetical tone, 'A few years down the line, you'll desperately want to quit this job that will have no charm left, and the sad part will be that you'll not be able to do so for doors to all other avenues would be shut by then and you shall have to serve Pan India Airlines till your retirement.'

The conversation did not progress further, as Mr. Gupte rose to leave for the world-famous red-light area of Bangkok – Pat Pong, which was a ten minute walk from the hotel. It was already night and as soon as we stepped out of the hotel, several seedy-looking men confronted us with albums full of scantily clad girls, trying to lure us to some place nearby. Mr. Gupte shooed them away and asked me to follow him. A short distance away, a world unfolded in front of us that was quite alien not only to me but to any Indian who hadn't visited Bangkok before. The small area was lined with bars playing music with fair skinned beauties skimpily clad in teeny-weeny bikinis, dancing on the stage. Menacing pimps however spoiled the ambience of the place, but Mr. Gupte seemed to be quite familiar with the area, and I followed him to a place called, 'Queen's Castle.' 'Here you should visit only the 'King's and Queen's Castles; they are safe and don't cheat you.' I wasn't however as sure for they looked similar to any other joint there but followed him nevertheless to a deck upstairs, climbing a revolving staircase. I had earlier taken his advice and kept only some small amount of money with me, leaving most of the cash and all my valuables like passport, credit cards etc. at the hotel, and I felt it was the right thing to do when one entered such sleazy joints.

We were seated on wooden benches, with totally naked girls gyrating on the stage in front. Mr. Gupte ordered a beer for himself and a coca cola for me, twitching the nipples of the naked girl who came to take the order. And instead of a slap, that I expected, the girl giggled. I focused my attention on to the stage, where the plain vanilla naked dancing was giving way to raunchier shows with the girls inserting all sort of stuff in their privates. I do not know why but a feeling of disgust overwhelmed me. Far from enjoying the show, I felt nauseated. 'I am not feeling well,' I told Mr. Gupte, who immediately sprang up, gulped the remaining beer from the glass, left a hundred bhat tip on the table and rushed out with me.

I felt better as we came outside.

'Are you ok?' Mr. Gupte asked me.

'I am sorry I spoilt your evening.' I said.

'Oh, no not at all, I have come here at least a hundred times, and the place has got nothing new to offer.' He said without displaying any displeasure of having to cut short an enjoyable evening.

'Thank you, Sir,' I told him wondering how one could go to that place a hundred times. In spite of the glitter of Bangkok, I could never forgive the Thais for treating their girls as chickens meant for slaughter. But then, memories of the brothel in Calcutta came back to my mind. 'Hapless women are exploited everywhere,' and that wasn't at all a happy thought. 'Women ought to be loved and respected and not treated as commodities. But that transformation in mindset will take ages, considering that most societies in the world are male-dominated. In a way, perhaps life for women is better in these countries than where they were forced to remain under wraps of veils with no freedom whatsoever.' I kept thinking about some rather heavy stuff on my way to the hotel.

As I was entering my room, Mr. Gupte said, 'You can get a girl in your room, just dial 4040, and you can pay at the reception.' I wondered, if that could be possible anywhere in the world – get a girl in a five-star hotel room, and pay for her services at the reception entirely legally. Of course, I didn't avail of the services, but headed straight to the fabulous bathroom for a hot water bath. 'Indeed Bangkok is an extraordinary city,' I mused lying in the bathtub with warm soothing water splashing all over me through a Jacuzzi faucet. At that point, I didn't know that more enthralling experiences of the other side of the city were awaiting me the next day.

We did not leave Bangkok the following day as scheduled since our flight was cancelled due to some technical reasons. Mr. Gupte had arranged for a day-long sightseeing trip that took us to the Buddhist temples, gardens and shopping centers. I was fascinated by the magnificence of the Reclining Buddha, the Emerald Buddha, and many other temples. I was amazed to know that there were over 40,000 Buddhist temples in Thailand. The tour ended with an unforgettable ferry ride on the Chao Phrya river. Mr. Gupte was a different person that day, telling me in depth about each temple and about the history of Thailand.

'You know, he said, 'the country's official name was Siam until 23 June, 1939, when it was changed to Thailand. It was then renamed Siam from 1945 to 11 May, 1949, after which it was again named Thailand. The word Siam could have come from the Sanskrit *yâma* meaning dark. The word *Thai* is not, as commonly believed, derived from the word *Tai* meaning 'independence' in the Thai language; it is, however, the name of an ethnic group from the central plains. A famous Thai scholar had argued that Tai simply means 'people" or "human being'. The Thai use the phrase 'land of the free' to express pride in the fact that Thailand is the only country in Southeast Asia that was never colonised by a European power.'

I listened to him with rapt attention, as he further enlightened me, 'Thailand has constitutional monarchy, and Bhumibol Adulyadej is the reigning King of Thailand. He is known as Rama IX. Having reigned since 9 June, 1946, he is the world's longest-serving current head of state and the longest-reigning monarch in Thai history.'

There were similar long lectures at the temple of the Reclining Buddha, where I was just swept off my feet at the magnificence and magnitude of it. 'It's called Wat Pho,' Mr. Gupte had informed me, and continued, 'It's named after a monastery in India, where Lord Buddha was believed to have lived. Prior to the temple's founding, the site was a centre of education for traditional Thai medicine, and it is where the techniques of traditional Thai massage that is used to cure a host of ailments even today, originated. Wat Pho is one of the largest and oldest wats in Bangkok with an area of 80,000 square metres and is home to more than one thousand Buddha images, as well as one of the largest single Buddha images of 160 ft length known as the Reclining Buddha.'

I was astounded by Mr. Gupte's knowledge which he downplayed saying that he learnt all this visiting Bangkok many times. I thanked Mr. Gupte profusely, which he politely acknowledged. I learnt a new lesson in life seeing Mr. Gupte – a drunkard and womaniser with a handlebar moustache need not necessarily be a bad person.

Next day, as I was putting on my uniform for the flight, I said to myself, 'Whatever Mr. Gupte may say, this is a fabulous job, and I am really lucky. I will never quit Pan India Airlines.'

Lord Buddha probably had smiled, for not too many days later; I had to quit Pan India Airlines. My life changed completely the day Ram Gopal Varma, one of the finest film directors ever, had boarded the flight between Maldives and Bombay, in which I was working in the Executive Class section of the brand new Airbus A320 airplane. I will come to that a little later.

ॐ

In a short while, I had visited a number of international destinations. Contrary to what the seniors in the vocation felt, I found the job to be very exciting. Though, to be honest, the flight pursers were a misfit in a profession that was more suitable for girls. In fact, we were a minority, and often at the receiving end, but I didn't mind. I was always treated as a cypher in school or college, unlike those who went on to get good marks, and so probably I was used to ill-treatment. The only time in my life that I felt like someone important was during my brief affair with Urmi. But that too turned out to be a tragedy. However, I had a job that I liked, which paid me a good amount of money, and at that point only that mattered.

But not just with me, life perhaps takes everyone on a rollercoaster ride of happiness and sorrow. On a typical working day, I was dressing up the trays in the front galley meant for pilots of the flight, as the last few passengers were boarding while a senior airhostess, Ms. Rakhee, was welcoming them the usual way with folded hands repeating expressionless *Namaskars*, like a robot. She was an attractive lady, but always had a tired look. I wondered why she never married, for it seemed from her conversations that she had always craved for a family of her own.

The last two passengers, a handsome middle-aged gentleman and his wife, an elegant lady had boarded, when I saw Ms. Rakhee's face go pale. She moved into the galley and pulled the curtain that put her away from any public view while I moved out to close and arm the forward entry door of the aircraft. When I entered the small enclosure which then had created a private space with the curtain drawn, I saw Ms. Rakhee sobbing. She tried to regain her composure, wiping her face with a tissue paper.

'Ma'am, aren't you feeling OK?' I asked her politely.

'No, I am alright, just feeling a little down. Can you find out where the gentleman and the lady who boarded last are seated?'

'Sure, ma'am,' I said as I walked into the aisle. I spotted them at once. They were seated right on the front seat of the Executive Class. The man was showing something in the in-flight magazine to the lady, who was looking at it intently. That they were a very happy couple could be gauged from a distance. I went back to the galley and told Ms. Rakhee about them.

'Can you find out their names from the passenger list?' she asked me.

'Sure, ma'am,' I said again, as I picked up the folded computer print-out of the passenger list from the crevice of the crew-seat. 'Mr. Ajay Pathak and Mrs. Tanima Pathak,' I read out.

Ms. Rakhee fell silent, and a little while later, called one of the airhostesses from the rear galley, 'Devina, can you work in front galley, I want to go back.' Devina readily obliged, and she came to work with me, while Ms. Rakhee quickly moved to the back of the aircraft. I saw her walking briskly, trying to avoid any eye-contact with the passengers seated in executive class.

I was a little surprised, for it was the norm that the senior-most cabin crew worked in the front galley to attend to the executive class passengers and to be able to quickly reach the cockpit in case of any exigencies. Ms. Rakhee was a stickler for rules and I couldn't fathom why she made an exception. 'Not feeling well,' couldn't be the real reason for workload in the rear galley was heavier than in the front. Of course, I didn't think it was appropriate to ask a senior crew member about her decision and kept quiet.

A few days later, I came to know the reason of such erratic behavior of hers, and felt very sorry.

Devina was a sprightly girl, who had got married to a co-pilot recently. Working briskly, she kept foul-mouthing the roster guy for not putting her on the same flight as her husband's.

'Yes, it's difficult to be separated even for a few hours, immediately after marriage I guess,' I said.

'Not that bro,' she said, 'that bitch Pompi is on that flight which my husband is operating. 'You won't know, how much I had to try to hook my husband and wrest him away from that bitch, who too was eyeing him.'

'Oh!' I had never thought of this angle, and her usage of a specific adjective every time she uttered the name of the other lady left no room for guessing as to how deeply she despised her.

I was relieved that service was to begin in the flight and she had to stop the blabber which I wasn't enjoying at all. Life in the confines of an airplane at over 30,000 feet above the ground had its moments of light and shade, elation and worries. That flight was otherwise uneventful.

I liked it more when I had a night-stop-over at a city other than in Delhi. Sleeping in a different city, and in a five-star hotel was any day better than sleeping in a room that resembled a war-zone between two bachelors. My room-mate's girlfriend too didn't show any of the qualities that a girl was supposed to have. Far from trying to arrange it a little bit, she made it even dirtier by throwing empty food packets, cigarette butts and beer cans here and there. On a day, when I had returned early due to an unexpected cancellation of my flight, and without the prior warning to my room-mate, I saw her in our room. She was wearing jeans but was topless. She showed no hurry to put on her top in spite of seeing me, and did so only after a bit of prodding from her boyfriend. I quickly changed my uniform in the bathroom and left in a hurry, much to the respite of my room-mate. I wasn't sure though if his girlfriend had other ideas for she kept saying that I could stay back if I wished. I, however, didn't choose that option not only because of moral reasons, but also for the fact that my room-mate was many times stronger than me. I certainly couldn't risk being beaten up. However, I had to admit that his girlfriend's figure was indeed fabulous, and the short duration that I had watched her topless gave me the stiffest hard-on in a long time.

However, once I got confirmed in the airlines and a fairly decent pay hike, the very next month I moved out of the sharing accommodation and rented a small one-room tenement in Gurgaon. It was much comfortable staying there all alone, but the rent was pretty steep. Spending all the money that I earned did not turn out to be a prudent idea, as I found out sometime later.

৩

As I was getting down from the airline car in the complex where I lived, a schoolboy confronted me, 'Are you a pilot?'

I thought of saying, 'no', but couldn't resist a bit of bragging, 'Yes.'

But much to my embarrassment, a girl, almost my age who was passing by said, 'No you are not.'

'Well, how do you know that?' I challenged her.

'I know,' she said. She pointed out at my badge at continued, 'Your badge is half-wing meant for flight pursers, and pilots wear full-wing badges.'

'Oh,' I was taken aback and said, 'yes, I am a flight purser.' The boy ran off making faces at me as the girl explained with a smirk, 'I'm a ground staff with Jetset Airways.' I decided to hate Jetset Airways since then as I hurried off to my flat. But like many of my resolutions this one too was broken within no time. I met the girl again the next evening. She was walking alone in the garden of the complex and seeing me said, 'Hi'. I tried to avoid her but she raised her voice and said 'hi' again.

'Hi,' I replied, not with the usual enthusiasm that a guy usually exhibits while greeting a girl.

'So you stay alone?' she queried.

'What a nosy girl,' I thought, and nodded in the affirmative.

'Then have dinner at my place,' she said and told me her flat number.

'Do you stay alone too?' I queried.

'Ah! That would have suited a bachelor like you, but it isn't the case. I stay with my Mom.'

I had a mind to decline her invitation, but then she said, 'well, you know I am a little outspoken. Don't mind all that what I say, but do come. We'll be waiting for you till eight-thirty. After that we'll lay the table and have dinner ourselves.'

I didn't say a word and returned to my flat. I wondered if it would be right to go to the house of unknown persons for dinner and that too after an insult. May be I would cook something swiftly. One of the first things bachelors should learn is cooking, my experience had taught me. You cannot have food from outside every day. And cooking isn't as complicated as it appears. There were some easy formulas that I learnt. For example, heat a little oil in a pan, put in some finely chopped onions and sauté them (but be careful not to burn), toss in some chopped tomatoes, add some spices like turmeric powder, cumin powder, a little *garam* masala and fry them till the oil starts separating. Throw in anything you like, chopped vegetables, fried fish and even chicken into it. Stir it at times; add hot water if it gets dry and cook till whatever you have put becomes tender. Add salt and sugar to taste (well, you'll know the proportions after watching a couple of Khana Khazana shows) and finally some chopped fresh coriander leaves and presto, you've cooked yourself a meal that is quite edible.

The first thing I did after entering the flat was to check the fridge. The fridge was almost empty. It would mean that either I had to go to the market to buy something to cook a quick meal, or eat the aircraft food that I had wrapped in a packet. I had always wondered how the air-caterers could make such horrible tasting stuff look so good. I opened the packet and was repulsed by the stale morning stuff of '*aghh*' food. I threw it into the waste bin. I bathed, changed, put on a liberal spray of perfume and went to the building where the girl lived. I hadn't even asked her name. But fortunately, she opened the door and smiled at me.

'Seven thirty,' she said, 'if Pan India Airlines was that punctual, even Singapore Airlines would have had to shut shop,' she said again with a smirk. She let me in and introduced me to an elegant lady, 'My mother. She is a Chief Cabin Crew with Lufthansa.'

Seeing the stunned expression on my face, the lady clarified, 'Well, Rittika was born when I was just 23, and now that she's 21, I still have 14 more years to go before retirement.'

'And before you ask about my father, let me tell you - don't.' Rittika said in her own matter-of-fact tone, 'he's gone for good, ditched my mother and left for the USA with his new lady love.'

'Oh! I am sorry,' I said.

'You needn't be sorry for that cheat,' she retorted inviting admonish from her mother, 'Ah Rittika, he's your father after all.'

Rittika didn't utter a word, but I could make out that some choicest expletives were running in her mind meant for her father.

'Human psychology is indeed strange,' I thought. 'Such a wonderful family, and why did that guy had to leave them!' My eyes went on to a photograph of three people, a young Rittika, her mother looking almost the same and a man standing in front of the Eiffel Tower. Another look at that man and I almost screamed, 'Is that your father?'

'Yes,' she said.

'Isn't he the famous Pandit...' I was stopped short of spelling out his name by Rittika's mother, 'yes, he is the world famous musician.'

There was no talk about Rittika's father thereafter. The dinner was fantastic and continuous chatter by Rittika and very dignified talk by her mother made the evening a perfect one.

'But I must warn you,' Rittika said during dessert time while her mother had been to the kitchen, 'you have to promise that you won't fall in love with me. Only then I'll be friends with you.'

I hadn't expected this from a girl on the first meeting, but reacted smartly and said with a chuckle, 'Eh, no one can fall in love with a girl like you.'

She got up and slapped me hard on my back. I hadn't expected this either, again on the first meeting with a girl. But she continued, 'then you don't know Rohan.'

'Rohan who?' I asked stupidly.

'Well, they are going to get married soon,' Rittika's mother who had entered the dining hall answered my query.'

'Well, what does he do?' I asked wondering if he was from the aviation fraternity too.

'He is a doctor based in Calcutta,' Rittika's mother replied.

'Oh! I said, but didn't make any further queries about him.

'And if you want to know how I had met him. Well, I had first met him at the airport, where he had arrived five minutes after his flight had left.' Rittika continued but thankfully stopped on elaborating on that. But it was easy to guess, a friendly Jetset Airways ground staff becoming friendlier with a handsome doctor after he had missed his flight and was visibly upset. They must have had ample time before the next flight to take off for a lifelong relationship. 'Oh! This could be easily dubbed as, love at first flight,' I thought out loud, inviting another slap from Rittika.

Rittika became a good friend of mine, and I cherished this relationship that came without any emotional baggage. I could share anything I wanted to with her, though I didn't quite feel free to tell her anything about Urmi. So I never mentioned her. Perhaps some secrets in a man's life cannot be shared with anyone.

Whenever, we were free she tugged me to a Café Coffee Day outlet located nearby and we had long chats.

'Which places in Delhi do you like most?' she asked one day and then it was revealed that though I had been living in Delhi for quite some time then, I hadn't gone around much to see the city.

'Oh! You've been a couch-potato then, I'll take you around Delhi. There's so much to see and feel,' she said. So, she took the responsibility of taking me sight-seeing, and I soon found out that Delhi is a fascinating city, a perfect blend of modern and the ancient. I fell in love with Delhi deeply and thought of settling there forever. And I was quite bowled over by Rittika's insight about the city.

'Well, how do you know so much?' I asked her sitting on a stone block in the Diwan-e-Khas of the Lal Quila or the Red Fort as she narrated the history of it. I had heard that the grand fort was built by Shah Jahan, the Mughal Emperor, but did not quite know that the peacock throne that was placed in the Diwan-e-Khas or the emperor's hall for private audiences was looted by the Persian king Nadir Shah or that the Marathas removed and melted the silver ceiling of the Diwan-e-Khas to generate funds for the defence of Delhi from the Afghan invader Ahmed Shah Durrani. Nahr-i-Bihisht or the 'stream of paradise' flowed through the centre of the hall. She had pointed to the arches at the corner of the walls that contained an inscription. She explained, 'It's the famous verse of the 13th century Sufi poet Amir Khushru, which reads— *"Agar firdaus bar rooe zaminast haminasto haminasto haminasto"* (*"If there be a paradise on the earth, it is this, it is this, it is this"*).'

'Wow!' I exclaimed and repeated my question, 'Well, how you know so much?'

'That's because I have a master's degree in history, besides one in hospitality management.' She replied with a giggle.

'What a girl,' I thought but did not say it loud.

Each day a Delhi tour with Rittika was a revelation in itself, and I was seemingly transported to another world hitherto quite unknown to me. On a night, shortly after a very tiring flight, when I slept off without even having dinner, I dreamt as if I was Shah Jahan seated on the peacock throne. A beautiful lady in Mughal attire came close, lifted her veil and whispered, 'I am Mumtaz.' As a flash of light brightened her face I yelled, 'You?' I woke up to find my T-shirt soaked in sweat and tried to close my eyes to catch the dream again, but in vain. For a long time, sitting on my bed, in bare torso I kept wondering why Mumtaz, the legendary lady for whom Shah Jahan had built the Taj Mahal, looked exactly like Urmi.

On my next day off from work, it was time to visit Lotus temple. The grandeur of the structure, and the philosophy of those who follow the Bahai faith, which welcomed people of any religion to pray inside the Lotus temple impressed me a lot.

Rittika told me to sit down on a bench and said, 'Pray, and you'll feel better.' She moved away from me, sat down on a bench at the far corner and closed her eyes. I looked around, soaked myself in the serenity and wondered what to pray about. I made general prayers asking God to bring peace on earth and eradicate corruption from our country. A tall order for God himself undoubtedly, but I made the prayers nevertheless. Rittika finished her prayers and joined me. On the beautifully manicured lawns of the temple, she went on with her lecture on the Baha'i faith, 'the Bahá'í faith is a monotheistic religion founded by Bahá'u'lláhin 19th-century Persia, emphasising the spiritual unity of all humankind. There are an estimated five to six million Bahais around the world in more than 200 countries and territories. In the Bahai faith, religious history is seen to have unfolded through a series of divine messengers, each of whom established a religion that was suited to the needs of the time and the capacity of the people.'

'Wow!' I repeated and said, 'Well, I am impressed.... more with your knowledge, than with the Bahai faith.' As usual she slapped me hard on my back, and I flinched. It did hurt a little, for the slap was quite solid.

Next on the list was Qutub Minar. Rittika had started lecturing in the auto rickshaw in which we were travelling. Auto rickshaws aren't quite the right vehicle to strike a conversation in. The noise around is overwhelming, and I had always wondered how a small vehicle like that could make such a ruckus. Besides, the openness all around invited dust and pollution. And if anyone had come across a polite auto rickshaw driver not just in Delhi, but anywhere in the country, I was willing to treat him to dinner at the Moti Mahal.

Qutub Minar, I knew was built by one Qutub-ud-din-Aibak, something that I had read in the history books while in school. But Rittika enlightened me with further inputs. I learnt that the minaret made of sandstone was the tallest in the country, and though the sultan ruler Qutb-ud-din-Aibek had started its construction in 1192, it was completed by the next ruler Iltutmish.

Since even going up to the first floor of the Qutub Minar was not permitted after the government banned it after a stampede in 1981, the other interesting monument that made me curious was the iron pillar in the compound. On that day, no one other than us was present there, which gave us ample opportunity to explore the place on our own pace.

'Stand with your back touching the pillar,' Rittika instructed. I wondered why, but complied with what she said.

'Now, try to embrace the pillar and see if both of your hands touch each other,' she came up with her next directive followed by a statement that was indeed remarkable, 'Well if your hands can touch each other, close your eyes, make a wish and that is sure to come true.'.

My fingers touched easily. It was easier for taller people, as the pillar tapered towards the top with its diameter reducing as one moved away from the base. I wondered what to wish for. Strangely it came naturally to me as I closed my eyes and Urmi's smiling face popped up in front of me. 'I wish Urmi loves me again,' As I stepped down, I mused, 'what a silly wish I had made, something that could never happen.' I sighed and looked out for Rittika. She was closely inspecting the intricate carvings on the Qutub Minar, lost in her own thoughts. I watched her from a distance. She was a wonderful girl, and very very knowledgeable. She had in fact altered my perception about girls. I had never come across a girl so deeply mad about academics. 'How would it have been if I fell in love with her?' I wondered, albeit the warning from her that she would stop being my friend if I ever thought on those lines. 'Let's go, it's getting late,' Rittika broke my thoughts suddenly turning around, adding as a rejoinder, 'you know, this Qutub Minar was probably named after Qutubuddin Bakhtiar Kaki, a saint from central Asia who came to live in India and was deeply respected by Iltutmish and not after Qutub-ud-din-Aibak as is widely known.'

'Oh!' I exclaimed, though my mind was far away from the era of Qutubuddins. I wondered if I had made one more mistake in my life. Embracing the iron pillar, I could have wished for Rittika's love, and that was perhaps plausible.

That night I deeply thought if I should propose to Rittika. True that she was engaged, and true that she had wanted only my friendship, but then people change, their attitude changes. That night I kept awake, thankfully there was no flight for me the next day. I slept off in the early hours of the day and dreamt again. I saw Rittika in my dreams strolling past the Taj Mahal and I rushed towards her with a bouquet of flowers in hand and a box containing a diamond ring. But as I came closer and she turned her head, I saw it was actually Urmi smiling at me. This time again, the dream snapped off immediately thereafter.

I woke up and sat on my bed for a long time lost in thoughts. It then occurred to me that I was not in love with Rittika, only that there was a deep liking for her. 'Let this relationship be friendship only,' I thought and ditched the idea of proposing to Rittika. That was probably the only right decision which I had taken till that time in my life.

A visit to Agra to see the famous Taj Mahal and Agra Fort was slotted for the next weekend. But the plan did not materialise as I had to attend some training session. And soon after, Rittika got married and left for Calcutta. I couldn't attend her wedding as my flight got grounded in Srinagar. I had told her that I would return well in time for her marriage. But it wasn't meant to happen that way.

It was one of my disappointing days. After all the passengers were boarded and seated and the doors of the plane closed I, like everyone else, expected the engines to start. However, the starting whine of the engines did not turn into a roar, and fizzled out shortly afterwards. The ominous voice of the captain came on the PA system, 'We have a small technical issue; please stand by for the next announcement.' But we learnt a little later that it wasn't a small issue. The engines weren't starting at all. The engineer, a nice guy named Sanjay, told the five cabin crew on board, after all the passengers were disembarked that the aircraft could fly back to Delhi only after a detailed inspection was carried out and rectification action taken. And that might take a while, since men and material were to be flown in from Delhi. I hoped that I would be able to take off at least the next day, just in time for Rittika's marriage.

All the crew members other than me were instructed to leave for Delhi by the next available flight. I was told to stay back in case they could manage a ferry flight, the two captains would require my service. I was the obvious choice as I was junior-most amongst all the other crew members.

I cursed my fate for I was desperate to be at Rittika's wedding. Repeated pleas to the higher authorities for permission to leave Srinagar and go to Delhi did not yield any results. In fact, a ground staff handed me over a print-out of a message that tersely said, 'NOT PERMITTED TO LEAVE STATION. NON-ABIDANCE WILL LEAD TO INITIATION OF DISCIPLINARY ACTION AND POSSIBLE TERMINATION FROM SERVICE. YOU ARE ADVISED NOT TO MAKE ANY FURTHER REQUESTS IN THIS MATTER.' I tore off the piece of paper and threw it into the dustbin.

Rittika was obviously disappointed when I called her from a public telephone booth to inform her of my predicament. But in her own spirited way she told me, 'Never mind, come to Calcutta sometime.'

I was put up in a tiny lodge near the airport, with bare minimum facilities. It was the month of December and bone-chilling cold outside. Thankfully, I had a couple of miniature Scotch whisky bottles in my kit. I had forgotten all about them and was delighted to find them while taking out my toiletries. I tore open a bag of potato chips to go along with the drink that I made to drown my sorrows. I took a long sip and looked out of the glass window of my room. It was a full moon night and the moonlight glistened on the icicles that hung from the sloping roofs of the houses all around, making it an unforgettable sight. The tall pine trees around were bathed in a soft glow, supplementing the mystic beauty of Kashmir. That they called this place 'heaven on earth' was no misnomer.

The knock on the door was just what I was waiting for. The room boy brought in a tray with a bowl of piping hot chicken curry and a casserole with warm rotis inside. He shut the door with a warning, '*subah tak aur kuch nahin milega.*' I nodded my head, checked that the water jug was full, for that could be the only requirement for me during the night and sat down to have my dinner. I quickly finished the frugal, yet delectable meal, pushed the tray out of the door, locked it from inside and poured the remaining whisky into my glass. I stood near the window, the moon had risen higher in the sky, shining brighter and enhancing the beauty of the night. The dim yellow lights from a far off hut's window added to that supernatural mood of the night. I stood silently with the glass in hand, and though it wasn't certainly the darkest evening of the year with the moonbeam's magical touch all over, Robert Frost's haunting poetry played back in my mind,

> *Whose woods these are I think I know.*
> *His house is in the village though;*
> *He will not see me stopping here*
> *To watch his woods fill up with snow.*

> *My little horse must think it queer*
> *To stop without a farmhouse near*

Between the woods and frozen lake
The darkest evening of the year.

He gives his harness bells a shake
To ask if there is some mistake.
The only other sound's the sweep
Of easy wind and downy flake.

The woods are lovely, dark and deep.
But I have promises to keep,
And miles to go before I sleep,
And miles to go before I sleep.

No, I didn't have to go miles before I slept, for in a few minutes from then I climbed on the bed, pulled the warm blanket over me and fell into a deep slumber.

The airplane remained on ground for a week. New engines had to be flown in from Delhi by a huge Indian Air Force aircraft named Gajraj. I had profusely cursed the aircraft engineers on the first day, pinning all the blame on them for the quandary. But soon my view about them changed. I visited the airport every day to watch the engineers and technicians work on the airplane. It was very cold, and snowing almost throughout the day. I had to admit that they were indeed the backbone of any airline company. I was deeply impressed by the way they carried out the work. Methodical and superbly skilled, the men on the tarmac deserved all the praise. The few days I stayed in Srinagar were the same, only that the Scotch ran out and was replaced by some *desi daru*. But I discovered that whether it was with Scotch, *desi daru* or nothing, wintry evenings in Kashmir was indeed surreal. I couldn't leave the lodge to venture out to the Dal lake or Pahalgam, as I could have been called to the airport anytime. But I promised myself that I would come back to Kashmir on a holiday soon and savour its beauty leisurely. However, that resolution too did not materialise in many years that followed.

I was very glad when the airplane finally took off from Srinagar. I was happy to get back to work and started with the routine job in the front galley. A complement of cabin crew was flown into Srinagar in an incoming flight. But for one Ms. Ranjana, all were junior to me.

After the aircraft was airborne and passenger service had begun, I heard a shriek. My senior and I rushed into the cabin to see a terrified young man on an aisle seat and a baffled newcomer, a petite girl in front of him.

'Yes Sir?' I enquired politely trying to figure out the reason of his distress. He didn't look like a psychic patient though. He pointed at his crotch where I found a bread slice lying. Accidently it had fallen flat with the buttered side down.

'Oh!' I wondered what to do about that as the new girl made another attempt to lift the slice of bread with a tong that she was holding. The man screamed again and covered his crotch with crossed palms. I stopped the girl, for her approaching the bread with the tong was rather violent. It would have been okay, had it not been resting on a most sensitive area of a man's body. Of course, any man would instinctively try to protect the area. I stepped in and gently lifted the bread slice with a tissue paper and threw it into the garbage bag.

'I'll make a complaint,' the man was furious though a short while after he cooled down, when two charming young airhostesses did their best to gently clean up the part of the trouser where the bread had landed with moist hand towels followed by dry ones.

Ms. Ranjana couldn't help giggling throughout the flight at the entire episode, and I too had joined her, making me feel quite relaxed after a rather depressing week that I had.

৪৩

Life went on its usual pace for a while after I came back to Delhi. There is nothing to mention about as such but for a stray incident that brought a smile on my lips. I was killing time at a bookstore in Delhi airport while waiting for my flight, when an elegantly dressed woman entered the shop. She caught my attention for she was looking for a book with particular thickness. That was quite an odd requirement but she explained to the sales guy after a while, 'Actually, one of my friends had borrowed a book never to return it. That has left an ugly gap in my bookshelf. I need to fill it up with a book of similar thickness.'

'Oh! In that case I would recommend you this book,' the sales guy handed over to her a book, and continued, 'Rudyard Kipling, and the book is bound in leather.' The lady seemed to be impressed but asked, 'Is it pure leather?'

'100% Ma'am, original from Australia,' the guy replied without any hesitation. He had made his sale though while checking out the lady asked him, 'What's Kipling? A type of game?' The guy smiled sweetly and replied, 'You'll find all the answers in the book itself.'

As the lady left, I couldn't help showing the sales guy the thumbs up sign. He came close to me and chatted with me for a while. I felt a little sorry for the guy for despite his MA degree in English; he couldn't manage to get a job commensurate with his qualifications and ended up as a salesman in a bookstore. But he said cheerfully, 'The perks of this job are enormous, you get to read the costliest of books for free.' I certainly learnt a little lesson from that guy that day on how to remain positive in life.

Rittika had left for Calcutta soon after her marriage, and I too moved out of the complex as the landlord wanted his flat back since his son was coming from the USA. I shifted to another rented flat in Rohini , owned by a pilot who was transferred to Calicut..

I was still a bachelor, and while mom's calls started including the topic of marriage as an end note, marriage was the last thing on my agenda for the near future. Somehow, I couldn't get Urmi off my mind totally. She was now married, lived in a different city and had kicked me out of her life. I shouldn't have been nurturing any soft corner for her. Yet…

'No Ma, I don't have an airhostess girlfriend,' I was getting fed up of repeating the same line whenever I had a conversation with her. Not many were interested in getting involved with a fellow worker for a host of reasons. But of course, I was to get married someday. 'Once I settle,' I used to tell her.

But things suddenly turned for the worse.

No, the shock this time around did not come from any heartbreak, but from the company that I worked for. Pan India Airlines was merged with Emperor Air, and that spelt doom for all the employees. I didn't understand much about the precarious debt situation of the company that everybody started talking about, but what happened after that was quite inexplicable. The company started paying salaries irregularly; often not giving a single paisa for months and I had a difficult time paying the house rent. Delhi is a city with very high cost of living, and I had been spending all my salary on rent, clothes and eating out. I had no savings to fall back on. Thankfully, unlike some of my colleagues, I didn't have any home or car loans. To add to the miseries, one

Mr. Hari Sadu was appointed as the Managing Director of the company along with one Mr. Bulldog from Croatia as his deputy. Both of them worked overtime to screw the happiness of every employee of the airline. Naturally, service deteriorated, lesser passengers flew and the company sank deeper into red. More and more money was spent on finding out ways and means to turn around the company, as a number of international consultants were appointed on fat salaries. They stayed in five-star hotels, zipped around in chauffeur-driven swanky cars and used up the remaining funds. They came up with a unanimous suggestion not to pay the employees their salaries for a year if the company had to be saved. They knew very well that airline jobs were scarce and everyone would pull on with their resources or by borrowing and would not be able to quit even if they wanted.

There were long inspirational letters from the Managing Director to the employees saying that it was only a matter of few months that the employees had to go without salaries, and advised them to manage somehow during these times. Several committees were formed to look into the employees' issues but all they did were to drain the company's money of whatever little was left and came up with absurd suggestions.

Like all other employees, the pilots were getting restless too. It was a sense of belonging to the company, and perhaps lack of jobs in the country that kept us going, but I wondered for how long. To add to my ill luck, one day Mr. Hari Sadu and his deputy Mr. Bulldog boarded the same flight from Delhi to Bombay on which I was working.

After take-off, Mr. Hari Sadu vanished into the front toilet for a long time, while I went to Mr. Bulldog, who was seated comfortably in his Executive Class seat and asked him courteously if he wanted tea or coffee. Mr. Bulldog was browsing through a magazine that I thought was Croatian 'Playboy,' and he didn't quite like my intrusion. 'Don't interfere,' he told me sternly. Oh! I forgot that he didn't like interference. In fact he had told none other than the Civil Aviation Minister not to interfere into all what he did, when the latter had asked for some details about the functioning of the airline. It was therefore perhaps natural for him to see interference from everywhere. I moved away thinking, 'Ok, if he needs any service he will press the call button and I will serve him then.'

As soon as Mr. Hari Sadu came out of the toilet, he headed straight towards the cockpit. The senior airhostess tried to stop him as the rule book said that no one was allowed into the cockpit of a flying airplane without the commander's permission. She told him politely, 'Sir, I'll just inform the captain over the intercom of your entry into the cockpit.' Mr. Hari Sadu flew into a rage.

'Do you know who I am?' he yelled.

The senior airhostess was taken aback, but replied politely yet firmly, 'I know that very well, Sir, but rules are rules.'

Hari Sadu shouted back at her, 'I am the boss of this airline, you are sacked right now – go to the Economy Class and sit there. Remove your uniform immediately. If I have given it to you, I can remove it as well.'

'Oh! This is a scene straight from the Mahabharata, when Dushasana tried to disrobe Draupadi by pulling her saree off,' I thought, as I stepped in to pacify him. 'Sir…' I had just started, but he nudged me aside and marched into the cockpit pushing the door open. The air hostess quickly vanished into the rear of the cabin out of sight of the megalomaniac.

Captain Bala, a very senior commander was in charge of the plane. He was an amiable, baldy and portly gentleman and I could see that he ushered Mr. Hari Sadu in as he saw him at the door of the cockpit. The co-pilot unfolded the observer's seat for him, where he sat down and began his rhetoric.

The cockpit door was closed for a while and I got engaged in work in the galley. With me alone in the front section, I had lots of work to do and then I heard the call bell from the flight deck. As I went inside the cockpit, I found Mr. Hari Sadu lecturing on what was needed to turn around the airline.

'What will you have Sir,' Captain Bala asked him. But he did not reply and kept on blabbering. Captain Bala repeated, 'Sir, tea, coffee, juice?' But Mr. Hari Sadu did not answer him but kept repeating, 'We have to turn around.'

'We have finalised TAP,' I heard him say.

'TAP?' Both the pilots looked puzzled. I too didn't quite get him, but he elaborated.

'Ah, as employees you should keep yourselves abreast with all the developments that are taking place in the company,' he said rather sternly and continued, 'TAP means Turn Around Program.'

'Oh! I thought it was some tap…' Captain Bala said, 'well that would ensure an uninterrupted flow of err…' he paused as the co-pilot completed, 'cash to us.' But Captain Bala commented, 'well I would like it to be Scotch,' and laughed out loud. The co-pilot joined him as well, and though I too was almost on the verge of laughing out loud.

'We have to turn around,' he said sternly and did not stop there. He got hold of Captain Bala's collar and shouted, 'Do you understand? We have to turn around.'

An exasperated Captain Bala gestured to the co-pilot Captain Manish, and by whatever experience I had about flying an airplane, I knew that we were returning to Delhi. Captain Bala announced over the PA system, 'Attention, ladies and gentlemen!

As per directives from our MD, we are returning to Delhi. He has instructed us that 'we have to turn-around.''

'Hey, what are you doing?' An irate Mr. Hari Sadu questioned Captain Bala.

'I am only obeying your orders, Sir,' Captain Bala replied sarcastically, 'We are going back to Delhi – you only told us that we have to turn-around.'

Mr. Hari Sadu flew into a rage and repeated the same line as he did with the senior airhostess, 'I am the boss of this airline, you are sacked right now. If I have given you uniform, I can take it back as well.' That seemed to be his favourite line when it came to dealing with employees of the company. But he didn't instruct Captain Bala to go to the cabin.

Captain Bala did not show signs of being upset. He said nonchalantly, 'You need not sack me Sir, I am resigning right now.' He took out a paper from his flight bag, wrote down a few lines and handed it over to Mr. Hari Sadu. He then alighted from his seat, went to the Executive Class section, removed his epaulets, sat down and started snoring. I started sweating under my collars. Of course, co-pilot Captain Manish would take us to Delhi, but this was the most bizarre incident that I had ever witnessed in my life. I stood frozen in the wedge between the commander's seat on the left side of the cockpit and the wall just behind it, which could squeeze in just one person. The cockpit door remained open, and so I could see what everyone was doing, both in the cockpit and in the front cabin.

Captain Manish had a terrified look on his face. Mr. Hari Sadu ordered him, 'You keep flying and land at the nearest airport. Thereafter, I'll see what I can do with obstinate employees.' But somehow his voice didn't have that strength as before, as he stammered a bit while passing on the orders.

Captain Manish did not talk back to him, but was seen communicating the same over radio. After a while, to my horror he got up from his seat and told Mr. Hari Sadu, who was still sitting on the observer's seat in the cockpit, 'Sir, our union has just declared a strike, and so I cannot work any longer.' He too went into the cabin and sat beside Captain Bala.

A airplane in the sky with none of the pilots seated in the cockpit was surely unnerving, and I could see Mr. Hari Sadu breaking into a sweat. I scurried out of the cockpit too, and thereafter something horrifying happened. The cockpit door closed behind, followed by a loud banging on it and Mr. Hari Sadu's yelling, 'Take me out, take me out, I agree to meet all your demands.'

A little while later, Captain Bala said to co-pilot Captain Manish grinning, 'I think that's good enough lesson for him, let's go, the aircraft won't be able to land on autopilot on her own.' But as they came to the cockpit door, there was a worried look on Captain Bala's face. 'Manish, do you remember the code to unlock the door?' Manish nodded his head and said, 'Oops, that's there in my notebook, but it's in the flight bag inside.'

It was time for us, me and the senior airhostess to get scared as well. Mr. Hari Sadu, who knew nothing about an airplane, was in the cockpit, and the men who were to fly it were locked outside the cockpit. The door could be opened by a switch from inside, or by entering a secret code on a pad from outside. The code was changed often, and was only given to the pilots.. The pilots looked at me helplessly, but no I did not know the code either.

Hari Sadu was getting restless, and banged the door hard from inside. Captain Bala shouted from outside, 'Ok Sir, since you have agreed to our demands, we will fly the plane, but we are unable to get inside as the door is locked. Do as we instruct you.'

Thereafter, Captain Bala tried to guide him as to which switch to press. But the door remained shut and the airplane made a sharp nosedive.

'Oh! Shit. I don't know which switch he pressed. I hope he hasn't disengaged the autopilot.' Captain Bala uttered exasperatedly. This time, both the pilots started sweating. The door was reinforced with steel bars and could not be broken either from outside.

Then I remembered something. I walked down the aisle and spotted an engineer. The engineers were amazing guys. They were usually reticent and not so impressive looking people but possessed enormous knowledge about airplanes. He looked at me quizzically, but when I asked him, 'Can you come with me; there is a problem,' he got up from his seat and followed me without a question. I escorted him to the cockpit door and asked him if he could do anything to open it. Quite obviously, he looked very puzzled, as he too was facing such a strange situation for the first time in his life. But he unlocked the cockpit door instantly by punching in the code on the lock-pad installed right outside the door. The pilots thanked him and rushed inside, and took over the controls, much to our relief. Mr. Hari Sadu came out of the cockpit looking ravaged as if a storm had passed over him. He quietly sat beside Mr. Bulldog, who had no inkling about the drama that had taken place, for he was sleeping soundly with the Croatian Playboy lying at his feet.

However, Mr. Hari Sadu did not keep his promise, which led to a full-fledged pilots' strike a few months later.

౮

I came across Ms. Rakhee a few days later on a flight to Kuala Lumpur again.

'Looks like there's some rioting in Kuala Lumpur,' the dispatch officer whom I met near the aerobridge was telling the other crew though he could not provide with more details. However, the flight was not cancelled, and the trouble at the destination station skipped our minds as the aircraft took off. On that flight I was the only male cabin crew member; the other five were all women. The flight was smooth, but upon landing, the handling agent's representative informed us that the situation in the city was tense, with army trying to control the rioters. A police van would take us to the hotel. On the way, we didn't come across anything untoward, except that the streets were totally empty.

However, at the hotel, we were faced with a dilemma. Since all the tourists were stranded, there was dearth of rooms. The receptionist girl told us rather harshly that six of us would have to manage in just three rooms that night. I looked at the women, and other than Ms. Rakhee, all were PYT types. I wondered if I would have to sleep on a sofa in the lounge. But Ms. Rakhee came to my rescue.

'Anurag, I don't mind staying with you,' she said and added, 'of course if you don't have any issues.'

'No, ma'am,' I said. Oddly, the other girls did not seem as relieved as I expected them to be. I could be wrong, but I felt a wave of disappointment passing over them though they did not say anything. 'It is not that I haven't stayed in the same room with a woman ever,' I thought and sighed, remembering Urmi for a moment.

The room that was allotted to us was nice, with two separate beds. Ms. Rakhee pulled out a vodka bottle as soon as we entered. She took out a soft drink from the mini bar and made drinks for both of us.

'We'll have a sip, freshen up and then ask for dinner.' she laid out her plan. I agreed with her. But it didn't go exactly as she had planned. She gulped down her first drink in no time and poured herself another one. She started talking while I listened.

'Anurag, you must prioritise your objectives in life,' she said. I nodded in affirmation, not quite getting her. By this time, I knew employees of Pan India Airlines never lost any opportunity to advise someone junior to him or her. But she changed the topic.

'You know I made only mistakes in my life,' she said, sounding a little tipsy.

'Everyone makes mistakes in life,' I consoled her with the best line that I could think of. But she kept telling her story, which I listened to intently.

'You saw that man Mr. Pathak on board that day?' She asked but did not wait for my answer and continued, 'I was going to get married to him. We were engaged, but just before marriage, I got this appointment as an airhostess in Pan India Airlines.' She paused for a sip but started off again, 'I broke the marriage to pursue this career. That time I felt it was the best thing to do. I wanted a glamorous life. It was always my dream to be an airhostess. When I saw those smart girls in uniform, I craved to be one of them. I couldn't just get into a marriage then, look after the household and raise children.' She again paused for another sip.

I opened a cashew packet brought from the aircraft and spread the contents on a plate. I picked up one and said, 'Ma'am you did the right thing. Early marriages are meant for those housewife-type girls.'

Ms. Rakhee went on to a pensive mood and said, 'No, maybe I didn't do the right thing. I couldn't find anyone as charming as Mr. Pathak thereafter. He was caring, he was educated and he came from a very rich family. His wife now moves around in an Audi, while I travel in a company provided rickety diesel Ambassador driven by a foul-smelling driver.' She emptied the glass and said, 'I miss having a family. I hate to go back to an empty room after duty hours. I hate to fall asleep drinking alone, watching stupid shows on TV.' After a brief silence, she then said out of context, 'You can use the bathroom first, I'll go after you.' I understood that she no longer wanted to talk about her life.

I quickly finished the drink, the first one compared to her third and went off to the bathroom. When I came out, I saw Ms. Rakhee in her undergarments, folding her saree neatly for the next day. The hotel had informed us that there would be no laundry service because of the riot. She went into the bathroom, as I dried myself and slipped into a night-suit. I ordered dinner, as she had instructed and switched on the TV. Horrifying scenes of rioting and shootouts were being beamed repeatedly. I surfed the channels and stuck to BBC for there was nothing worthwhile to watch elsewhere.

Dinner was served by the room service boy after a long time, but Ms. Rakhee was still in the bathroom. I knocked on the bathroom door, but got no reply. I felt concerned and turned the knob to find the door unlatched. I saw Ms. Rakhee lying naked in the bathtub with her eyes closed. Thankfully, her head was above the water. I shook her, and she mumbled something. As she was slipping into the waters, I had no option but to lift her from the bathtub. She was not in her senses, but wrapped her arms tightly around my neck. I placed her on the bed. Strangely, even with a naked woman in my arms, I did not get any amorous feelings. I dried her with a towel, and covered her with a sheet. I then tried to bring her to senses by rubbing a wet handkerchief repeatedly over her forehead. She responded soon and got up on the bed and I heaved a sigh of relief.

She apologised profusely for the trouble. 'I don't know it happens at times, when I just cannot wake up after a few drinks. I am extremely sorry.'

'Not at all Ma'am,' I told her.

'Call me by my name,' she said.

'Yes Ma'am,' I replied as she smiled over my not abiding her instruction. She dressed up quickly, and sat down for dinner. Dinner talk was confined to the company and generally badmouthing the bosses.

We were tired, and slept off quickly on our respective beds. When I woke up next morning, she already had bathed and dressed up for duty. 'Finish your chores, while I make tea,' she told me, and assured that there was no hurry as such, for the pickup transport would come only after two hours.

The return journey was uneventful, and as Ms. Rakhee bid me good-bye at New Delhi airport, she said, 'Thank you *bhaiyaa* for all that you have done for me.' I felt sad for her as she disappeared behind the sliding doors of the arrival lounge. 'Life, more often than not, is a betrayer.' I thought pulling my trolley-bag towards the exit.

*****

5

KIS MOD PE A A JAATE HAIN...

One of the troubles that came along with an airline job was the security check everywhere. At times, I felt that those guys were overdoing things. It certainly made no sense to confiscate an earthen pot of *rosogollas* from a well-known singer or to tell a pilot to remove his belt. One of the exasperated pilots had once told a security man, 'If I want to hijack an aircraft, I can fly straight to Karachi. I need not carry a pistol with me.' But that led to more questioning from the security men, with the pilot ending up apologising, 'I shall never loose talk or ever go to Karachi on my own.' He even gestured to hold his ears and do sit-ups. The flight that he was operating naturally got delayed though the real cause wasn't revealed to the passengers. They were told that it was due to some operational reasons.

But, in spite of the security checks and all the hoopla associated with them, there was a real hijack that changed my life. It was on the day when Ram Gopal Varma had boarded a flight on which I was working, as I had narrated earlier.

A few days earlier, there had been a false alarm. One guy got up from his seat on the plane and shouted at the top of his voice, 'Hijack.' No sooner he did so; another guy sprang up from an aisle seat, took out a gun and fired at him. However, it went blank, and as all heads turned to him, he said embarrassedly, 'I am an Air Marshal, employed to protect the aircraft from any hijack threat, but I don't know how the gun failed me.' One passenger took the gun from him, inspected it and said, 'Oh! Chinese stuff, no wonder.' It was time then for the hijacker to come out of his shock and yell, 'I am no hijacker, I was just saying 'hi' to my friend Jack at the rear of the cabin.' An equally baffled man came forward, and said as he hugged his friend, 'Thank God for the Chinese that you are still alive.' Everyone was relieved, and settled down for the flight.

The Chinese did the right thing – gave the world good food but sub-standard guns. I didn't know why, but the fabulous lunchtime buffet spread at the Mainland China restaurants crossed my mind when I should have been more worried about the situation around me.

But a few days later, on the flight from Maldives to Bombay, there was an actual hijack situation. As I stood at the front entry door to welcome the passengers, the famed film director Ram Gopal Varma boarding the flight caught my attention. But also spotting two suspicious-looking men behind him made me a little uneasy. I however, chose to ignore them and looked around to see if an entourage of film personalities was following him. No, he seemed to be travelling only with an attractive lady acquaintance. I thought of going up to him to ask how much I enjoyed his films *Mast*, *Rangeela* and *Satya* but restrained myself.

But the drama in the air started soon after. One of the suspicious looking men got up from his seat as soon as the 'Fasten Seat Belts' sign went off with a 'ting'. He took out a pistol and said in a chilling voice, 'This is a hijack.' I was moving down the aisle when he pointed the gun straight towards me. I stopped instinctively with my hands up in the air just a row away from the seat where Ram Gopal Varma was sitting.

'Some kind of a drama by the *filmwallahs*,' I thought, but I was mistaken. Another man got up from his seat with a long knife in his hand. He too blurted out that it was hijack and everyone ought to remain quiet.

I stood still, trying to gauge how many of them were there. 'Only two,' I concluded, after running a visual check on all the passengers who were seated on the aircraft. The horror stories of an earlier hijack in which the hijackers had taken the aircraft to a god-forsaken place flashed in my mind. I felt like crying and thought; 'Now they will take us to some place like Gobi desert, where we won't even find water for ablutions.' The man with the knife moved forward menacingly and stopped right in front of me, exactly beside where Ram Gopal Varma was seated. At that point, I don't know what it was, but something took over me. I kicked the man hard in his balls, snatched the knife from his hand, and threw it with all my might towards the man with the pistol, all in a flash. The knife cut his hand and the pistol fell off. I sprinted down the aisle and collected the pistol in one swift move. Leena, a well-built air-hostess who was watching it all from behind, hit the hijacker with a steel coffee jug right on the head. Another air hostess did the same thing with the other one. Thereafter, the passengers gathered to tie the two hijackers to two seats on the back.

The commander of the aircraft, Captain Gopiraj, came out of the cockpit, patted my back and said, 'Great job bro, I watched it all on the close circuit TV in the cockpit.' Thereafter, all the passengers broke into a huge applause for me. I felt quite embarrassed. The icing on the cake was that Ram Gopal Varma got up from his seat, hugged me tightly, took out his visiting card and gave it to me saying in an emotional voice, 'You have saved my life, come to me for anything.'

Upon landing at Bombay, I didn't know how the media came to know about the incident but they thronged the arrival lounge armed with cameras and microphones. Some passenger who had filmed the entire episode with his mobile phone camera had forwarded the clipping to a TV channel as soon as we landed, and they had already started beaming it. As reporters surrounded me, someone put a garland around my neck, while a few lifted me up and shouted slogans, 'Anurag Sen *zindabaad*.'

But things did not turn out to be as what I had expected. I was soon called for an internal enquiry by Emperor Air officials. I thought that the board comprising of a dozen-odd personnel would be praising me for my bravado that saved the aircraft from a hijack and perhaps recommending a promotion. But it was far from that.

The afternoon I was called to attend the enquiry, I was seated outside a boardroom for a couple of hours, as I watched tea, coffee, fish fry and chicken cutlet being carried into the room by caterer boys. I was called in by an office staff rather rudely and I entered the large rectangular boardroom with a number of officials in suit and ties seated around an oval table. The frowns and grimaces on their faces made me feel as if I was a criminal and not a hero. The interrogations started shortly afterwards, once the chairman of this board, a top shot from Engineering Department, whom I had never seen before finished his snacks. One of the board members introduced him, 'He is Mr. Vishal Sharma, and he is a non-vegetarian.' Well, that surely was an odd way to introduce someone, and I wondered if being a non-vegetarian counted as a qualification. In these situations, you have no option than to simper, nod, and accept all types of stupidity without any argument. I did the same, and faced him managing a feeble smile. He looked even more ferocious than the hijackers and began by blurting out at me, 'Do you know what you have done? You put over a hundred lives in jeopardy.' He then went on to explain to the board, 'If the gun that the hijacker was carrying went off accidentally, and it had pierced the roof and if …' I shut my mind, and stopped paying attention to his blabber, though I felt I should have brought my earmuffs too. Thereafter, a flight safety officer took out a rule book and narrated some 'relevant' paragraphs as to what had to be done during such a situation. Kicking on a hijacker's balls was not written in that book and so he concluded that I had violated the safety rules of the company as well. Each of those guys in tie and suit took their turn to condemn my action in the air. Only one gentleman tried to argue in my favour, 'But the boy has done a marvelous job. If the airplane was hijacked and taken to a foreign land, we would have faced a lot of trouble.' But his voice was drowned by the protests from all others. Finally, a personnel manager, who seemed to wake up from his sleep passed on the judgment, 'You are suspended till further enquiry.' He ordered me to hand over my identity card and made me sign a paper which stated that I had done a severe offence and that during the period of my suspension, I wouldn't be paid any salary. I wouldn't be able to work anywhere either. I wondered, if they wanted me to die of starvation. But it was futile to argue with them, and they showed no signs of relenting, in spite of my breaking down and begging them for mercy. They laughed loudly, and one of them commented, 'Aha, you should have thought before showing off your *herogiri*.' I now knew why every grassroots-level employee hated the management of Emperor Air. They were sadists, who would get jealous over any employee's success and did their bit to pull him down.

I was devastated. I didn't know what to do. From that day onwards, every day I made several rounds to the various offices of Emperor Air, but in vain. The only moments of joy came in when I was conferred with some awards from various governmental agencies. Even the Honorable Civil Aviation Minister gave me a certificate of appreciation. Most of the passengers on that flight had also sent me costly gifts stating how grateful they were to me. All that gave me a sense of pride, but those were hardly anything to run my household. Though I was single, paying for food, rent and other essential stuff cost quite a lot in Delhi.

No one from Emperor Air really did come forward to help me. My colleagues were threatened by the management of dire consequences if they helped me in any way. My parents too had retired from their services by then, and I just couldn't tell them that I was suspended from service, for only a few days back they kept telling me over phone how proud they were of me, after seeing me on TV after the hijack. I ran out of money, and even those who knew me, stopped talking to me for fear of having to lend some money. The fear was quite unfounded though, for my sense of self-respect did not permit me from borrowing money from anyone.

But after several months into the suspension, on the day when I had only the money left to buy a couple of day's meal, I decided to meet Ram Gopal Varma in Bombay.

ॐ

Coincidentally, I got a phone call from a clerk in the Operations Department, informing me of the subsequent hearing that was to be held in Bombay the very next day. That suited me fine, for it meant free air travel from Delhi to Bombay and of course free breakfast on board. However, after reaching the office, where the hearing was scheduled, I was told that the person in charge would not be coming as he was indisposed and I would have to come on a later date about which I would be intimated in due course.

I took out some money from the ATM at the airport, discovering to my utter delight that my father's add-on credit card still worked. 'Parents are parents; they are the only ones who come to your rescue during times of need,' I thought.

Locating Ram Gopal Varma's office that was called 'Film Factory' in Juhu was a breeze. The auto-rickshaw driver, after dropping me to Varma's office, asked me if he should wait for me to take me to Amitabh Bachchan's bungalow as well. He seemed disappointed when I declined his offer.

Ram Gopal Varma was a very busy person, and I wondered if I would be able to meet him. He could be away for a shooting or on a holiday. I came without an appointment and to be honest, an apprehension did cross my mind that he could deny ever meeting me. After all he came across so many people every day. But to my sheer luck, as I entered the office, Ram Gopal Varma himself had just come out of his cabin to talk to someone. He instantaneously recognised me. He came close and gave me a big hug and said in an emotional voice, 'Brother, it's so nice to see you.' He took me to his garishly decorated cabin with posters of his films all around. I didn't waste much of his time and came to the point quickly.

'Sir, can you give me some job?' I said.

'Aha! Another one bitten by the film industry bug,' he said getting up from his chair and patting me on my back. I didn't elaborate as to why I desperately needed the job, but he added, 'Job? I'll make you the hero of my next film.'

That was an offer for which I wasn't prepared for and said, 'No, Sir, let me work in this industry for some time and learn how to act.'

'Ok, as you wish,' he said, asking me where I was staying.

'I've just come by the morning flight,' I said, mentally calculating if the money I had in hand would suffice for renting a room in a guest house for a few days.

Ram Gopal Varma thought for a while, took out a key from a drawer, handed over to me and said, 'I have a small furnished flat in Borivali, which is lying vacant. You can stay there if you want.'

I thanked him profusely, for this was indeed God sent and took the key with as much politeness possible, for I felt like snatching it from him.

Thereafter, I was dropped at the flat by a chauffeur-driven Mercedes.

I sank into the plush backseat of the swanky car and got immersed deep into my thoughts, as the car struggled to negotiate heavy traffic on the Western Express Highway. Calcutta wasn't kind to me, neither was Delhi. I wondered what Bombay had in store for me.

I opened the flat, as directed by the chauffeur of the car, who had escorted me to the lobby of the building. It was a small apartment but well decorated and with all amenities like fridge, TV, microwave oven and all. I thanked Ram Gopal Varma again and again loudly.

I joined Ram Gopal Varma's production house as an assistant, and soon found that I loved the film industry which is a confluence of money, glamour, creativity, passion and talent. And every moment in the film industry was exciting.

I made a quick trip to Delhi to wind up my settlement there.

I sent my resignation to Emperor Air and never again heard from them.

∞

Years passed and while working with Ram Gopal Varma, I graduated to an assistant director. I simply loved the job, for each day was different and exciting. I met a man named Joy Jolly and true to his name, I have never come across a funnier chap than him. He supplied various equipment and manpower to the film industry. We soon became best of friends. One day while we were having a drink in a Versova bar, he came up with a proposal.

'Anurag, I've watched you work. Can you make a film all by yourself?' he asked.

'Yes, why not?' I sounded confident, but said, 'But making a film requires a lot of money. Even a small budget one will require a couple of crores.'

'OK, Anurag, I always had this dream of producing a film. I can probably finance a small budget film.' he said finishing his drink and preparing to get up. He never exceeded three pegs, come what may. He left, bidding me good-bye as I told him that I would leave a little later. I kept sitting there alone, trying to get the proposal to sink in, and idly watching the rather unattractive girls gyrate to the tunes of latest Bollywood chartbusters on a low stage close by. I had a couple of drinks more, and then staggered out, hired a cab and returned to my apartment. By then, I was thinking of the apartment as my own. Ram Gopal Varma's secretary, of course, deducted a fair amount towards rent and handed me my salary thereafter. Honestly, the salary wasn't that great and I barely managed to cater to my needs.

Next day I went to Ram Gopal Varma and told him about Mr. Joy Jolly's proposal.

'Sure, go ahead, but I thought of casting you as the hero of my next film. I gave a stupid smile and said, 'Sir, Akshay Kumar will be a better choice.'

'Oh, how many times have I told you to call me Ramu and not Sir; and wish you all the best. And in case your film flops, the hero's offer will still be valid,' he said.

Joy Jolly and I started working on the film immediately with the cast of an entire set of newcomers. We of course could not afford Saif Ali Khan and Kajol, as our lead though they would have fitted the script to a 'T'. We looked out for some new faces to act in the lead roles.

'There is a girl named Soma, whom you can take as your lead female character.' Joy Jolly told me a couple of days later.

'OK,' let's call her for a screen test' I said and queried, 'does she have any acting experience?'

'She's an aspiring actress, a small-time model. In fact, tomorrow there's a fashion show at the Mariott Hotel and she's going to walk the ramp. Of course the star of the show will not be her, but the other well-known models Praneeta, Laila, and Angana. Let's go there, I've got two passes.' Joy Jolly replied.

Next evening, we got ourselves seated in the front row seats, a few feet away from the ramp. That was the first time I had been to a fashion show. In spite of being in the film industry for quite some time, I had never had the opportunity to witness one before.

I watched with rapt attention as the girls cat-walked wearing weird dresses. I wondered if anyone would ever buy those garments to wear in real life. A dress that had a tail-like thing hanging, another had holes in them and so on. There was an entourage of photographers and videographers around, but everyone around seemed to be quite bored. I caught a few of them yawning as well. Then, a very graceful girl caught my eye, and when she came on the ramp wearing a green chic *saree* Joy Jolly whispered in my ear, 'She's Soma.'

'Yes, she'll be good for the heroine's role,' I whispered back.

Just as she left the ramp, there was short break when we went backstage. Soma was more attractive than what we felt from a distance. She was intelligent and receptive, and when we explained the reason for our meeting her, her eyes gleamed in anticipation. She agreed instantaneously to our proposal. We fixed up an appointment in the coffee shop of Holiday Inn the next day for an elaborate discussion and signing up. Though she was a newcomer, I had an inexplicable feeling that she would make it big someday.

After the break, we took our seats again for the remaining part of the show, as Soma told us that she had a final cat-walk towards the end. We wanted to watch her poise once again. As the show started, I noticed an unexpected change in the attitude of the photographers and videographers. All of them suddenly became very attentive, and placed their cameras at strategic locations. Ms. Praneeta, who was somewhat well known, came on the ramp wearing a long robe. All the photographers started clicking incessantly and the videographers let their camera roll non-stop. I wondered what was that they found so attractive in her. She was neither very pretty, nor was her dress gorgeous. But then she suddenly stopped at the middle of the ramp and in that jerk, her robe fell off. She stood there completely naked for a while, but quickly gathered her aplomb, picked up the dress from the floor, wore it to cover herself fully and completed the walk as if nothing had happened. She waved at the crowd and vanished backstage.

'Tomorrow onward, she will be famous,' Mr. Joy Jolly commented.

It was indeed so. The wardrobe malfunction story hit the headlines, and in spite of the TV channels and newspapers having to blur her boobs and pubic region in the pictures, she became a household name overnight. I was not sure if all of it was pre-planned, but then I had learnt that in show-business, everything was possible.

Next afternoon, we finalised our contract with Soma. She was indeed very beautiful, with hypnotising eyes. I wondered why she wasn't picked up by some renowned director earlier. But I knew that in the film industry, innumerable talent and beauties ended up playing just one amongst the countless extras all throughout their lives.

Shooting of the film titled, *'Jeevan Ke Safar'*, started shortly. During the course of the shooting I came to know more about Soma and her struggles in life. It was a heroine-centric film and the story was based on a novel by Sharat Chandra Chattopadhyay, but adapted to modern times. The black rotary phones were replaced with mobile ones; the heroine wore jeans and T-shirt in place of traditional *saree* and so on, but the drama was in place. The film was turning out to be good and we were hopeful that it would do well at the Box Office.

Soma was indeed fabulous and she did go on to become one of top heroines later. But her story will be part of another book of my experiences in the tinsel town. And I can assure you that it will be more interesting than this one.

৪১

However, a disaster that I had never envisaged struck me. I was dumbfounded and shell-shocked when one fine morning I heard of Joy Jolly's death. He had passed away after a massive heart attack during his sleep. The film was almost complete with just a few scenes left to shoot before going on to the editing table. At his funeral, I broke down and sobbed inconsolably. People around gave me surprised glances, for his wife too didn't look very sad over his demise.

I scouted for finances to complete the film, but without any success. Joy Jolly's wife shooed me away, in spite of my rhetoric that she should fulfill her husband's dream. Ramuji was out of the country and as it is, he himself was going through a rough patch and I wasn't sure if he could have helped me with funds. All the financers I met did not want to risk their money on a rookie filmmaker. Soma and the entire cast, comprising mostly of newcomers, became very anxious as well. They too, like me, were banking heavily on this film for their careers to take off. I didn't know what to do. My dream was so close, yet so far. I started getting into depression that led to excessive drinking. I started doing strange things.

One day I took a train to Dadar station, and on a whim took a bus to Goa. I had nothing on me, not even an extra set of clothes and little money in my purse. I reached Goa that evening and went straight to Arambol beach hiring a motorcycle taxi. I sat on the beach drinking beer purchased from a shanty nearby. It was a full moon night and the foamy waves that splashed the beach glittered like tiny diamonds. The moonlight shimmering on the sea with twinkling lights from distant ships made it all look like an enchanted place. I looked up and cried, 'Oh! God, shall I always be a loser throughout my life?'

I was startled by a voice from behind. I saw a bearded naked man and a naked lady, both of whom were foreigners. 'Come with us,' the man said, 'and you'll feel better.' I followed them to a hippie camp nearby. A campfire was lit and naked men, women and children danced around it. Someone passed on a *chillum* to me. I took a deep drag and went in a trance.

The few days I stayed with the hippies thereafter till my money ran out, gave me an insight to their lifestyle and philosophy. I shall detail that out too in my next book as part of my Bollywood life story. But one of their ideologies did impress me.

A very old man, told me, 'Our tribe is on the wane. The hippie subculture was originally a youth movement that arose in the United States during the mid-1960s and spread to other countries around the world.' And amongst many other information that he provided about the hippies, one that was very thought-provoking was what he told me about their disliking for clothes, 'You know clothing is the first step towards discrimination. You wear a better dress from your brother and there it creates a difference. And we are part of nature. God never send you to the earth with clothes. Did he?' He had a point there, but roaming around naked in Churchgate, Bandra or Thane was certainly not an acceptable proposition. No, I didn't quite agree with him, but he did admit that in the modern world it was not always possible to do without clothes.

I came back to Bombay hitch-hiking, as I was totally broke. I took a local train from Andheri where a nice couple had dropped me in the final leg of the journey to Bombay and managed to travel to Borivali station without ticket circumventing the ticket checkers. Thereafter, I walked the remaining couple of kilometers down to my apartment.

That evening I went to a *filmi* party, only to get free booze. I wasn't invited, but one of the cameramen who was invited, and could not attend due to some personal engagement, gave me his invitation card. The poolside party at hotel Grand Maratha was quite impressive, with who's who of the film industry walking in. I could see them all, Salman Khan, Katrina Kaif, Aditya Pancholi, Vivek Oberoi… the list was truly long. I took a drink, went to a dark corner and sat there. No one spoke to me. No one noticed me either. After the first quick gulp that almost half-emptied my glass, I focused my attention to the typical Bollywood dance show on a stage in front with Cyrus Broacha and Archana Puran Singh as anchors sending the crowd roaring with laughter. I was perhaps the only one in the audience who wasn't laughing. I silently sipped the whisky from my glass. I felt very depressed and dejected. And when one is depressed and dejected, he does exactly what Devdas did in Sharat Chandra Chattopadhay's novel– he drinks beyond his capacity. I could feel the fifth peg numbing my senses, the alcohol making its way into the cells of my brain, clouding it. But, I was disconcerted by an announcement when I reached for another peg.

'Ladies and gentlemen, we are proud to present before you, the sponsor of this gala party – Mr. and Mrs. Aditya Agarwal, owners of India's largest snack chain – Roomino's – get hot *samosas* and *kachauris* delivered to your rooms, just call…'

I hadn't paid much attention to the long advertisement that followed, but yes Roomino's was beginning to be a household name that delivered piping hot Indian snacks home within no time. I had tasted their wares, and yes their '*Sampurna Samosa*,' or '*Idle Idly*' were indeed lip-smacking stuff. I looked around for some snacks to go along with my whisky.

Then I heard the next announcement, 'Now, a few words from Mr. and Mrs. Agarwal…' There was a round of applause. I wasn't focusing my attention on to the stage as I was trying to locate a waiter, when the voice over the loudspeaker stunned me from deep inside. It was a voice that I had heard before, and then it struck me that Aditya Agarwal was my very friend Mote.

I heard him speak in fluent English, asking everyone to enjoy the party to the fullest. Then he announced, 'I would request my wife Adwitia to say a few words.' He handed over the mike to an attractive lady and seeing her I got the shock of my life. She was none other than Mrs. Dhol.

As a publicity stunt, Mrs. Dhol, oops Mrs. Agarwal, sang a few lines of a song, with Mote joining her. I heard Mote's sonorous voice after many years and it made me very nostalgic. It was too much for me to take in one evening. I called for the waiter, and downed two quick pegs of whisky. I knew I had far exceeded my capacity and decided to leave the party. But as I staggered towards the exit, I could not hold myself steady and blacked out. The last thing I remembered was that the towering personality of Indian cinema, the ever respected and loved Mithun Chakravarty, was holding me with his strong hands. He prevented me from falling on a skimpily-clad starlet. Mithunda seated me on a sofa as a few of the waiters rushed in. I could hear all sorts of ignoble comments around, '*Sala koi ayre gayre party mein ghus jaata hain,*' '*Saale ko dhakka marke nikalna chahiye…*' the word '*sala*' being repeated in every sentence. It was just like as it happened many years ago in another five-star hotel in Calcutta during Urmi's marriage ceremony. But I somewhat came back to my senses when someone poured a jug of water over me. I heard Mote's voice then, 'Who is he?' and some waiter's reply, '*Koi faaltu aadmi, saar, abhi nikal dega,*'

But then as I was trying to get up from the sofa, I saw Mote staring at me. For a moment he stood still, then let out a shout that startled everyone in the party.

'Guruuuuuuuuuuuuuuuuuuuu.'

He hugged me tight, astonishing everyone around. I fainted in his arms again.

ॐ

When I woke up next morning, I came to the conclusion that I must be in heaven. I was lying on a huge bed with floral bed-sheets in a big tastefully-decorated room, overlooking the Arabian Sea. I sat up on the bed and pinched myself. No, there was no indication that I was dreaming or that I was dead. Just as I was wondering what to do next, a petite young nurse in blue uniform entered the room.

'Where am I?' I asked her.

'At Mr. Agarwal's apartment in Juhu, Sir,' she replied and continued, 'You are otherwise fine, just a little drunk last night.'

'Drunk?' I thought out loud.

'Well, the doctor who had visited you last night said so,' she replied, and asked, 'you must be hungry, Sir?'

Yes I was, but I needed to wash, go for the other morning chores first. As I rose from the bed, I noticed that I was wearing a fresh new night-suit and not the two-piece suit and tie that I had worn to the party.

'Who changed my clothes?' I asked the nurse.

'I did, Sir,' she replied unhesitatingly. I kept quiet in embarrassment- a young lady removing the clothes of a drunken man wasn't a happy thought, particularly if the man happened to be your own self. I went to the bathroom and couldn't help exclaiming, 'Oh! What a bathroom!' I had a long bath and felt refreshed. I wore the new set of clothes presumably kept for me on the rack and came out to find a couple of servants wheeling in a trolley full of goodies – toasts, eggs, butter, jam along with flavored Darjeeling tea in an exquisite bone china teapot. I sat down on the sofa and picked up a toast and started buttering it – I felt famished anyway and thought, 'Let the dream last as long as it can.' However, within a few minutes I had another surprise in store.

Mote walked into the room along with his wife.

'Guru,' did you have a good sleep? he asked.

I nodded and held Mote's hand, 'Thank you Mo… err… Aditya, for all that you have done for me.'

'What Guru? What are you saying? You have saved my life thrice, and I have done nothing for you. And Guru please keep calling me Mote – it sounds nice.' I wondered if I had saved Mote's life thrice, but during the course of long conversation that followed, he reminded me of the first meeting with him, when I had saved him from the bullies, and then when I saved him from drowning. That would have been all, but he said focusing his eyes at the distant horizon and very slowly, 'Guru, you had saved not just me, but Adwitia as well when you stopped that asshole from circulating that video.'

'Oh!' I exclaimed softly and thought, 'I never knew Mote had such a sharp memory.'

Mrs. Mote, (well, she told me to call her that) laid the breakfast on the table and during the most memorable breakfast of my life, Mote told me his story. Mote had asked Mrs. Mote (then Mrs. Dhol) if she would marry him immediately after the video incident, when he left the New Town College. Mrs. Mote was a bit hesitant at first because of their age difference, but Mote had a long list of names right from celebrities like Sachin Tendulkar (Abhishek and Aisharya weren't married then) to lesser mortals like one Krishnendu Chaudhury (a senior and topper in his school who went on to become the head of Google in India), who had married women older to them.

'Kurt Russel was five years younger to Goldie Hawn but they got married, Audrey Hepburn, though older by seven years had married Robert Wolders and Gina Lollobrigida had married a guy who was 34 years younger to her!' Mote informed me triumphantly during the narration and I had to admit that in spite of being a member of the film fraternity, I never knew all that. I learnt from Mrs. Mote that it hadn't taken much persuasion on the part of Mote thereafter for she was fed up with her married life and she had mused, 'Why not take a chance? It cannot get any worse from this.'

Mrs. Mote, oops her name was Adwitia (that literally meant second to none) came from a very rich family but her parents had died in a plane crash when she was a child. Her uncles had usurped their property and almost forcibly got her married to Professor Dhol, whom one of the uncles knew. She was just 18 then, while Professor Dhol was over 40. However, even after her marriage, she managed to complete her graduation in Chemistry. She was beautiful, educated and yet confined in a cage of sorts. Well, she didn't have any children, because Professor Dhol was impotent.

'Ah, this is absolutely filmy stuff,' I thought, but did not speak my mind.

Mote and his wife opened their hearts to me, as if I was part of their family. We sat chatting throughout the day. Thankfully, it was a Sunday, and they didn't have to take the day off.

For Adwitia to get married to Mote wasn't difficult at all. Soon after they had eloped, Professor Dhol had committed suicide, saving her the trouble of going through a complex divorce procedure. Mote's father too had suffered a massive heart attack and passed away after a few days of their marriage, ostensibly for not being able to accept his only son marrying a married woman. But doctors had said that the cause of his death was his high cholesterol and blood pressure. Whatever it was, Mote now became the head of the business that he had inherited. Adwitia wooed Mote's mother and became very friendly with his sister Aditi and even managed to get her separated from a vagabond show-off type of a boy with whom she was going steady. She got Aditi married to a handsome lawyer with promising future. Well, let me not get into those family matters of Mote, for then it would be another Ekta Kapoor '*saans, bahu, dewrani*' serial and the size of this book would even surpass Vikram Seth's 'A Suitable Boy,' which the low cost publisher surely would not permit. Mote also told me that they had a son, who was studying in Rishi Valley School and stayed in the hostel.

After marriage, Adwitia didn't become another typical Marwari housewife attending *bhajan* sessions and eating all the stuff fried in pure *desi ghee* and making her butt round and rounder till it resembled a basketball, but assisted Mote in his business. In fact, Roominos was her idea. She had argued, 'If the Dominos guys can make it big by selling pizzas, which Indians don't really crave for, there is no reason why a home delivery start-up serving *garma garam samosas*, *kachauris*, and *dosas* wouldn't become successful.' The tagline, 'Happiness *ki* room delivery,' was very similar to that of Dominos and was coined by Mote. 'Deliberately done,' Mote confessed. 'Anyone thinking of eating a pizza is bound to have a second thought – both the brands are equally visible, and you get six *samosas* for the price of one veg pizza,' he explained. After a pause, he said in a hushed tone but with a wink, 'And make double the profit in the process.'

I nodded my head in amazement and thought, 'Indeed, how a simple business model has made Mote so rich.'

'What's up with you Guru?' Mote asked then.

My story was longer and as I told them all, I noticed Mrs. Mote's eyes moisten at times, though she quickly composed herself. I concluded by telling them about my unfinished film.

Mote thought for a while and asked, 'How much do you require for finishing the film Guru?'

'About a crore or so,' I replied, making a mental calculation of the work that was unfinished.

'Just a crore?' he seemed surprised.

'Yes,' I said, wondering how rich Mote was then to make such a princely sum of one crore sound as if it was small change.

'Guru, you finish the film, I'll finance it.' Mote said and looked at his wife.

'Of course,' Adwitia said, seemingly excited about the project.

'I have just one request,' Mote said. I looked up to him as he hesitated to spell out.

'Guru, if you can accommodate a song sung by Adwitia in the movie,' he said finally.

'Of course,' I said marveling over the love and bond that existed between them after so many years, whose relationship anyone would have discarded as shallow and dismissed to be just an infatuation at one point in time.

But that is the enigma of love – it obeys no set formula, it follows no fixed track.

౸

With Mote's money, I managed to complete the film. As the day of its release drew close, I became very nervous. I prayed that it should recover the costs at least, though Mote had assured me not to bother about the money that he had invested in the film.

'Mote isn't expecting the film to do well for he had already given up on recovering his money,' I thought as I walked down the full stretch of Juhu beach one morning. Though unlike the beaches on the east coast, the grandeur of sunrise with the sun popping up from the blue seas, painting the frothy waves orange, was not visible from Juhu beach, morning was the only time when one could at least walk somewhat peacefully. Though the menace of horses trotting past was curbed by the police, the presence of a huge crowd, vendors and seedy characters made the place quite unfit for an evening walk. However, morning walks too did not come without the hazards. With people's pet dogs dirtying the beach. An attractive girl in shorts with a cute spaniel running close to her heels disrupted my thoughts for a while but the anxiety came back soon.

'I have always been a loser,' I thought. 'What to do next?' I wondered. Going back to Ramuji for work was the only option left after that. I touched Ramuji's feet in my mind. 'He is my Godfather,' I thought. There was only person in the whole world on whom I could fall back upon. Of course Mote had come back to my life, maybe he could give me the job of a manager in one of his stores.

I had been calling up my parents once in a while. They had sold off the house in Calcutta and shifted to Hyderabad to permanently settle there. I had told them that I had quit Emperor Air as I got a better opportunity in Bombay, but they did not seem to be very convinced. Mom did not harp on the topic of marriage anymore, for perhaps she could gauge that I wasn't in a position to get married.

But miracles do happen and at times life smiles at you. The film that I made was released on a Friday, the thirteenth, which changed my life completely.

'It's a good film,' most of who viewed it said after the screening of the premiere show at Fame. Honestly, I felt it was a wonderful film. But then everyone perhaps felt the same way with their creation.

After the show, there was a small party in the banquet hall of an ordinary hotel. Mote and Adwitia could not attend due to some other engagement. But the cast and crew, who felt that the film would be a blockbuster, were present. I could make out that they were speaking from their heart and that made me feel good. For the first time in my life, I was being congratulated for something that I had done.

I wished Urmi was here with me. That was wishful thinking, I knew. She was married long back. I tried to count the years – nine, ten, eleven... may be more. How time flew. And I wondered why she came to my mind, when in the film world I was always surrounded by attractive damsels. Did I still love her? I didn't have the answer.

Soon guests started leaving and it was time for me to leave as well. On my way, sitting on the rear seat of a taxi that took me back to the flat in Borivali, I wondered where life would take me from there and if I would just vanish into oblivion if the film totally flopped.

'In that case,' I concluded, 'Urmi did the right thing by not marrying me.' And I wondered again, as to why Urmi came back into my thoughts frequently.

However, the film became a surprise super-hit, and won accolades both from the junta as well as the critics. The Indian audience was perhaps starved of a movie with a good storyline and melodious songs. Oh! I had to admit that the music director, Preet, and the singer duo, Ishan and Chhanda, did fabulous job. They indeed infused life into the film. I must make a special mention of

Adwitia, whose only song, a ghazal that I had included at Mote's request, was also very well received by the audience. And last but not the least, Soma gave a mind-blowing performance and became a star overnight.

The critics compared my film to *Anand, Amar Prem, Golmaal, Chitchor* and the likes, classic family entertainers of yesteryears. But I was glad that the film did very well, making me a hero in the process. Producers lined up to make films with me, and I became one of the most sought-after directors.

The film gave me enough money to buy a small flat. I bought a Hyundai Elantra, and harboured the thought of buying an Audi after a few years. The thought did make me wonder as to how the level of greed increases with success. A few years back, buying a car was nothing but an unrealistic dream, and now even thinking of an Audi did not seem that preposterous.

Before starting next feature film, I chose to do a documentary on Geeta Dutt and Guru Dutt. I didn't know why I was so obsessed with this couple – Geeta Dutt's voice, her failed marriage to the eccentric Guru Dutt, his tragic end and everything. Undoubtedly, they were one of the most talented couples in the film industry ever. Yet, what tragic lives! Geeta Dutt died at the age of just 42 of liver cirrhosis caused by excessive drinking and Guru Dutt, on all probability had committed suicide at the age of 39. But no one can ever forget *Saheb, Bibi aur Ghulam, Pyasa* or *Kagaz ke Phul* that Guru Dutt made or the songs like '*Ei sundor swarnali sondhay, eki bondhone jarale go bondhu…*(in this beautiful evening in what bondage have you entangled me friend?)' sung by Geeta Dutt. Geeta Dutt was a Bengali, I came to know. She was born as Geeta Ghosh Roychowdhury and one among the ten children of *zamindar* Debendranath Ghosh Roy Chowdhury who migrated from East Bengal to Calcutta in the earlier forties, and then shifted to Bombay in 1942, where Geeta Dutt started her singing career. The making of this movie required a lot of research, but this time around, funds were not a problem as a number of corporate houses came forward to sponsor it.

One evening, as I was listening to some unforgettable songs on my Bose system, sitting on my armchair in my newly acquired flat in Ekta Meadows in Kandivali, the phone rang. I let it ring till Geeta Dutt stopped belting out, *'Babuji dheere chalna, pyar mein zara samhalna…'* I simultaneously pressed the answer button of my mobile phone and the pause button of the music system.

One of my agents was calling. He had some information about a few unreleased songs of Geeta Dutt in the possession of a collector of Calcutta. I decided to go to Calcutta by the early morning Emperor Air flight as Geeta Dutt 's voice filled the room, *'tabdeer se beegdi hui takdeer bana le, aapne pe bharosa hain to dao laaga le.'* So very prophetic, so very provocative! Yes, 'go ahead; take that gamble in life, if you have confidence in yourself.'

It was the first time since I left Emperor Air, which seemed to be ages back, that I boarded an airplane. It felt nice to be seated in the 'J' class of a spanking new Airbus A321 aircraft. I felt a bit nostalgic as memories of my days as a flight purser flashed back in my mind. I looked around. The 'J' class area that could seat 20 executive class passengers was almost full.

I was seated by the window. A fine young man came and sat on the vacant seat beside me. 'Hi, I am Atin,' he said. I nodded and smiled at him. It was a long flight and I struck a conversation with him. He was a very impressive person and I developed an instant liking for him.

'Sir, you've made a wonderful film,' he had said. I was further enthralled to know that his wife Ujani had worked for Pan India Airlines for a short while. I, of course, did not disclose to him at that time that I too had began my career with Pan India Airlines.

At Netaji Subhas Chandra Bose International Airport, Atin's wife Ujani had come to receive him. She waved at us from the steel fencing that separated the conveyor belt area and the arrival hall. She waved at Atin who was walking alongside with me and I was absolutely startled seeing her. She had the same poise, same wonderful eyes as Urmi, only a little younger. Later on, I became very close to the wonderful couple and when they heard the story of of my life, they had exclaimed in unison, 'Incredible!'

'Sir, you must publish your story,' they had said. And sometime thereafter, Ujani had called me and said, 'Sir, I am sending an author from one of India's largest publishing houses Srishti to you. He was after me to for a story of an air-hostess, but I am sending him to you, for I feel a novel based on your life will be much more interesting.'

I was in a dilemma if I should be telling everyone my story, but could not turn down Ujani's proposal. So, here it is. I hope readers like it.

ॐ

Going back to my story, after I bid good-bye to Atin and Ujani at the Calcutta airport, I got in a chauffeur-driven Mercedes that was waiting for me, courtesy Hotel Sonar Bangla, where I was booked for two nights. I had offered Atin and Ujani a lift, but they had thanked me and said that they had their car in the parking lot. I went straight to the person who had those masterpieces of Geeta Dutt. The man, an ex-employee of HMV, lived in the northern fringe of Calcutta at a place called Sodepur. He parted with the 78 rpm records of Geeta Dutt, only a few of which were released somewhere in the late fifties for quite a paltry sum of few thousand rupees, an amount much lesser than what I had expected. And as I was leaving, he grinned stupidly and said, 'I have copies of the songs on a CD.' I nodded and thought, 'What a fool he is,' and left thanking him. As I climbed into the cool and comfortable interiors of the Mercedes, I felt very happy about the successful mission.

The Mercedes traced the roads of Calcutta, which made me to travel back in time. The journey brought back many memories and I became very nostalgic. I told the driver to go via Esplanade, a place which I used to frequent during my school and college days. I walked along the footpath adjoining the Grand Hotel. Everything was the same, the same stream of locals moving about, the vendors selling the same wares on footpath, the same sales pitch ... 'asun, asun...er thheke sasta aar paben na kothhao...come, come, you won't get it cheaper anywhere else.' Then I went to Park Street, a short distance away and had lunch at Tung Fong, where I had brought Urmi once. I sat on the same table, which we once shared for a dinner. 'Calcutta has a certain old-world charm, nothing changes here for a long time,' I thought. Tung Fong was exactly the same I had seen over ten years back. 'Ten years?' I mused, 'may be more.' I tried to recollect the date as I fiddled with mixed chowmein on my plate with a fork. Everything seemed to have frozen in time, only that I missed someone sitting with me. Suddenly, I felt very sentimental and my eyes moistened. I got up, paid the bill and left, much to the surprise of the waiters. The manager came running and asked, 'Wasn't the food alright, Sir?' I assured him, 'The food is great, only that I am not feeling that well,' I somehow managed to excuse myself out of the restaurant.

I decided to go back to the hotel and relax there the rest of the day. The chauffeur was glad, for he thought that after dropping me at the hotel, his duty would be over. But things did not quite turn up like that, and that day proved to be another turning point in my life. Ironically, the car stereo at that time was playing Kishoreda's evergreen song, '*Yeh jeevan hain, is jeevan ka, yehi hain, yehi hain, yehi hain rang roop, thhore gam hain, thhore khusiyan, yehi hain, yehi hain, yehi hain chhao dhup...* 'yes, indeed 'this is life with its myriad colours, little sorrow, little happiness, the shades and the lights...'

The car got stuck in traffic because of a fairly large procession of traders who were demanding some tax roll-back. It moved at snail's pace, as I lazily looked out of the rear-seat window, suddenly my eyes crossed something that made me sit upright. I rubbed my eyes, and no I was not wrong.

The lady walking briskly down the footpath was Urmi for sure. She was wearing a cheap saree, with no makeup or ornaments. She looked tired and withered. But in spite of all that, her beauty was intact. She boarded a bus just ahead of my car. She obviously didn't see me. That's the advantage of being inside a car with tinted glasses. And usually, pedestrians never watch out for those who are in cars.

'Follow the bus,' I instructed the driver. He obeyed without displaying any displeasure. He had been used to the whims and fancies of those who hired his car. He followed the bus that seemed to be on a never-ending journey. I told the driver to halt at every bus stop, so that I could see where Urmi was getting down. Finally, she got down at a bus stop near Patuli, a predominantly middle-class locality on the southern fringe of Calcutta. As she walked into one of the by-lanes, I got down from the car and followed her being very careful not to get spotted. That wasn't as difficult as I thought, for she never looked back and walked straight. The afternoon sun added that golden tinge to her charming figure. I fought with my emotions, attempting with all my mental strength to seal those feelings that tried to erupt like a volcano and force me to run to Urmi.

I watched her from a distance, as she went inside a small house with a tiny garden in front. I walked a little closer, and noticed the name-plate outside. Only one name was written, 'Urmi Banerjee.' I was sure that it was where Urmi stayed, but I wondered what had led to her living in such penury, and reverting to her maiden surname Banerjee. I could recall that she was married to one 'Chattoraj.'

I thought of going inside but could not muster the courage to do so. I went back to my hotel, and wondered what to do next. I decided to go to Urmi's house next morning. I had to meet her, not with any expectation, but just to see her once. And that evening, lying on a comfortable bed of one of the most luxurious hotels of the country, it occurred to me that I still loved Urmi dearly in spite of all the insults that had been inflicted by her, in spite of her betrayal. .

It was midnight when I called up Mote. Adwitia had picked up the phone and said instantaneously, 'So you found your love?'

'How did you know that?' I was very surprised.

'Well, women have this sixth sense you know,' she giggled.

'OK, I'll hang up now, there's no point in waking up Mote now,' I said.

'Oh! How do you know that he's asleep?' she queried.

'Men too do have some sort of a sixth sense,' I said, not disclosing that I could hear Mote's snoring over the phone.

My mind drifted back many years, when I had stayed at Mote's home one night on the pretext of studying together. But we hardly studied as Mote slept off and started snoring soon after dinner. We were in first year then, and I had looked up to the starry, moonless sky and wondered about my future. Urmi hadn't come into my life then. Those were the days when one pondered about the future, but wasn't excessively worried.

'How time flies,' I wondered looking at another starry but moonless sky many years later from the glass panes of Hotel Sonar Bangla.

∞

There were a few curious onlookers as the Mercedes made its way into Urmi's neighbourhood the following day. Yes, residents in these localities didn't quite expect ritzy cars in the vicinity. It was around ten in the morning, and the autumn weather was just perfect for a meeting of old lovers. I was apprehensive though. I didn't know how Urmi would react. 'Women are like the stock markets. No one can correctly predict them,' I thought. If she created a ruckus, I could be beaten up, in spite of my designer suit and chauffer-driven Mercedes. It was the city of Calcutta, after all. But I had to meet her, whatever were the risks involved.

Hesitantly, I pressed the button of the door bell outside the small house. An elderly lady, presumably a maid servant opened the door.

'Is Urmi at home?' I asked her politely.

'No,' she replied promptly, but added, 'Urmi Madam leaves for school at eight in the morning.'

'Oh!' I couldn't help expressing my disappointment and prepared to leave. But I turned around hearing a young boy's voice, 'Who is that, *Masi?*'

I could see a young boy seated on a wheelchair who had wheeled himself to the door. He looked at me and said, 'Mr. Anurag Sen, you can come inside and chat with me for a while.'

I was somewhat surprised and queried him, 'Eh, how do you know my name?'

'You are on all TV channels these days,' he replied as a matter of fact.

I didn't know what had attracted me to this boy, but I went inside. The outer room was tastefully decorated with simple and cheap furnishing and artifacts. I seated myself on the cane sofa-set and looked around. The boy was sweet-looking, and his legs didn't seem as if he was inflicted with polio.

'Hi I am Anurit,' he introduced himself and continued, 'you must be wondering why I am confined to a wheelchair?' He paused a bit but before I could react said, 'There's a problem in my spinal-cord, that has paralysed my legs. But I am fine otherwise.'

'Oh,' I said and it occurred to me that the boy was pretty intelligent, a little over-smart for his age though.

And he was talkative as hell. In the next few hours, I learnt almost everything that I was wondering about Urmi. I learnt that he was 12 years old, and that his father Mr. Deepak Chattoraj had died when he was just two.

The maid servant provided me with all the other information, after I had given her a Rs. 200 tip, while the boy was away in the bathroom.

I felt very sorry for Urmi over what I heard from the lady.

Within nine months of her marriage, Urmi had given birth to her son. The marriage wasn't a happy one, as Mr. Chattoraj was short-tempered and often beat Urmi over silly matters. Just after the boy was born, Mr. Chattoraj was charged for some fraud by the bank where he worked. It came into light then that he was having a torrid affair with a secretary in that same bank. Mr. Chattoraj was sent to jail, and Urmi's parents, perhaps propelled by a feeling of guilt over getting their daughter married to the groom of their choice, did everything to get him out. It was not known then, but revealed later on that Urmi's parents had borrowed huge amounts of money to pay the lawyers, bribe higher authorities and so on to get their only son-in-law out of jail. He did come out on bail finally, but not before Urmi's father had died after a sudden massive heart-attack. Urmi's mother passed away soon after, and after his release from jail, Mr. Chattoraj never left home and spent all his time drinking. Urmi took up a teaching job in a school that paid meager amount, and had a tough time keeping the various creditors at bay.

It was not known if it was accidental death or suicide, but Mr. Chattoraj was found dead on his son's second birthday. A concoction of sleeping pills and alcohol were attributed to his demise. Urmi had to sell off her parent's house to pay off the loans. Thereafter, she had purchased a small piece of land at the outskirts of Calcutta with the remaining money, and constructed that small house where they lived.

As I was struggling in life, I had often cursed Urmi, calling her betrayer and all that. I had imagined her to be a contented woman leading the usual happy family life - movie and dinner out on weekends, a holiday abroad every year just as they showed in Country Club ads. I never knew that she suffered too, and so very deeply. More often than not we make assumptions that are far from reality. Perhaps, each and every time we think, 'Oh! Why does this happen to me?' we ought to think that something worse is perhaps happening to someone else. I felt ashamed of what all I had thought of Urmi.

'Shall we go to Mainland China for lunch?' I asked Anurit, who had now come out of his bath. I wondered how he managed to bathe himself all alone. I expected a 'no' for a reply, but he replied enthusiastically, 'Sure, but mom shouldn't know,'

I lifted the boy and placed him carefully inside the car. The glint in his eyes showed that he was very happy.

'I am coming out of the confines of home after a very long time,' he revealed.

'Enjoy yourself,' I said. He held my hand tightly and then released it without saying a word.

On our way to Mainland China, Anurit informed me that his condition was curable with an operation, 'but,' he said, 'Mom doesn't have the money.'

Both of us had a wonderful time at Calcutta's most posh shopping mall, South City. Wheeling him around, I was quite consumed by a sense of divinity. I wanted him to buy some clothes, but he refused.

'Well, what would I tell Ma, if she asks where I had got them from?' he asked.

I did not insist after that, for he did have a point there.

I dropped Anurit back at Urmi's house. She hadn't come back from school yet, and I didn't wait to meet Urmi that day. I left for the hotel, after a fulfilling feeling, something new for me too. Honestly, I wasn't sure how Urmi would react on seeing me and I didn't want the boy to get any drubbing. It would have been natural; no mother would have wanted her son to go out with a stranger. And I didn't want to spoil my mood that day. On getting back to the hotel I called up my producers to tell them that I would like to do some shooting in Calcutta. They had readily agreed. That day itself I moved in a serviced apartment, there was no point in taxing the good producers, though they had told me that I could stay at Hotel Sonar Bangla as long as I wanted.

I went back to Urmi's house again the next morning. Urmi had left by then as usual, but this time around I wasn't sure if I was keener on meeting Anurit or Urmi. I had felt an instant bond with the handicapped boy, and I didn't quite fathom why. The computer in his room was his best friend. He studied, played, listened to music and did all he wanted to from his work-cum-play station.

'I told Ma not to send me to school anymore,' he started tapping on the keyboard and said, 'In Calcutta it's not easy for a child of my condition to move around. May be the rich can afford that, going to school by car and all that.' He paused, keying in some more data into the computer. 'And there is no need either; I can learn all what they teach in school and more from home. This Internet is an amazing technology.' He enlightened me.

I nodded in agreement though I had little knowledge about Internet technology.

'You want to see something?' he asked me.

I was curious and nodded in the affirmative.

With the help of the mouse and the keyboard he went to my bank's site. I couldn't quite guess what he did, but he opened my account's page in no time.

'Oh! You've got lots of money in the bank,' he said forebodingly.

I waited for his next move and then saw with horror that my account balance deplete to almost zero. Simultaneously, I got a SMS message that said, 'An amount of Rs. 43,00,000.00 debited from your account towards online transfer to xxxx xxxx xxxx 5990'

I let out a yell, but the boy was unfazed. 'Where did the money go?' I shouted.

'Chill, it has gone to my mom's account. She has just Rs 40,000 in the bank, some hundred times less than what you have,' he said coolly.

'*Saala*…,' I yelled again and it screamed in my mind, 'just a fraudster like his father.' I wondered what the boy would be when he grew up. But the boy was unperturbed and said, 'Aha, no bad words please.' That seemed to pour kerosene to the fire of anger inside me that was then in flames. Had the boy not been physically challenged and confined to a wheelchair, I would have surely slapped him.

I rushed to the door to head for the bank's nearest branch. As soon as I reached the door, I received another message on my BlackBerry, 'An amount of Rs. 43,00,000.00 has been credited to your account by online transfer from xxxx xxxx xxxx 5990.' I heaved a sigh of relief, but decided to leave for the day. I anyway had to go to the bank and do something to protect my money.

'How did you do that?' I asked the brat as I prepared to leave.

'So simple,' he smirked and that again fanned the fire of anger in me that had somewhat subsided after seeing the money back. But I controlled my emotions and restrained myself from an outburst. He continued, 'Well, when you were paying for the buffet at Mainland China with your debit card, which you had pulled out from behind a Swami Vivekananda's picture, I noted the username written on it. And strangely your password is 'Urmimylove7' which is scribbled on the top white portion of Swami Vivekananda's picture. You shouldn't do that buddy.' He passed on a sermon like a savant.

'Oh!' was all I could utter. I was at my wit's end and didn't know what to say. I left hurriedly.

As I stepped out of the house I came face to face with Urmi who had just closed the garden gate behind her and turned around.

I froze. For a moment a whirlwind of emotions swept all over me. I was standing in front of Urmi, my long lost love and couldn't speak a word. For a 35-year-old man that was certainly odd. For someone who was a filmmaker, it was even strange. But it happened to me. I stood there motionless, speechless.

Urmi took a step forward and looked at me. The expression on her face was placid and did not reflect any of the emotions that I was preparing myself to confront with – anger, disgust, horror. There was just tiredness and a hint of sadness in her beautiful eyes.

I stood paralysed as Sir Cliff Richard hummed in my mind,

> *Fall in love, fall in love, fall in love with you,*
> *Fall in love again, fall in love again,*
> *Why couldn't I, or why shouldn't I fall in love with you?*
> *Please give me one more chance, this is my first romance…*

'You can come in and have a cup of tea,' she said softly. I fought the biggest emotional battle in my life to overcome the urge to hold her in my arms, but could not fight the tears. I didn't know if she noticed the droplets roll down my cheeks as I wiped them off with the cuffs of my shirt, just being able to murmur, 'Another day,' as I rushed to the parked car.

Next day I reached Urmi's house before she left for school. The maid opened the door, and ushered me in. Urmi was in the bath and she didn't know that I had been seated. I couldn't see Anurit, and presumed she had taken him along for a bath. I was right. The maid said, 'Madam has taken Baba for a bath, she loves him a lot. And why not, he is the only one in the whole world whom she can call her own.' She sighed. I fiddled with my BlackBerry. Soon, Anurit emerged looking fresh after a bath, powdered and in a freshly laundered dress, carting his wheelchair.

'Hi buddy,' he greeted me.

'Who's there?' Urmi shouted from the bathroom and as I glanced towards the bedroom inadvertently, the curtain flew in a gush of wind, and through a mirror placed on a corner that reflected the ajar bathroom door for a flash of a second I watched Urmi's silhouette, as she shut the door almost coinciding with Anurit's shout, 'The famous film director Anurag Sen.'

'Tell Masi to give him some tea', she instructed.

I heaved a sigh of relief. She didn't discard me after all.

Urmi came out after a bath dressed in a robe with intricate stitch designs, looking fresh and beautiful.

'When are you leaving for school,' I asked her the first question in many many years.

She smiled and replied, 'Schools in Calcutta are usually closed on Sundays.' Oh! I started my conversation with a blunder. It totally skipped my mind that it was a Sunday that day.

'Have lunch with us today,' Anurit requested me. 'Ma is a fabulous cook,' he added.

I looked at Urmi wondering if she was endorsing that too.

'We would love that,' she said with genuine interest, after a pause probably wondering if I would agree to the invitation.

'But let your mom not cook today,' I said, 'we'll ask Bhojohori Manna to deliver something at home.' I had heard about the delicious Bengali dishes that this new chain of restaurants served, and Anurit and Urmi agreed to the proposal instantaneously.

Over delectable lunch of *chingri malaikari*, a prawn dish cooked in coconut, *mangsher korma,* a mutton dish cooked with cashew-nut paste, and other fabulous items promptly delivered at home , tor the first time in my life, I felt that the setting was complete – good food on a dining table surrounded by a man, woman and child.

I had to leave immediately after lunch. There was a phone call from a technician at the studio in Tollygunge where they wanted to discuss some of the points about my shooting schdeule. As I left, both Anurit and Urmi stood at the gate to see me off.

On my way to the studio, I wondered how life had come to a full circle, indeed. '*Zindagi ke safar hain yeh kaisa safar, koi samjha nahin, koi jaana nahin…*' Another unforgettable Kishoreda song lip synced by the superstar Rajesh Khanna that aptly described my feelings was being belted out by a radio at a nearby *paan* shop as the car had stopped in traffic. I thought of my life, which seemed to be nothing short of a film script. But then perhaps everyone's life has a story with its ups and downs, sorrows and happiness, the highways and the alleys, the straight roads and hair-pin bends.

I had already started weaving a dream with Anurit and Urmi. So what if the boy wasn't mine and I despised his father? How could I ever forget the slap from him on Urmi's marriage day? Unfortunately he was dead, or I would have probably slapped him back, or could I? Time and success does make one forget past animosity.

I was satisfied with the arrangements made in the studio for my shooting that was to begin the next day. The agent in charge of my work was a smart fellow who introduced me to Prosenjit, perhaps the most celebrated Bengali actor after Uttam Kumar and Soumitro Chattopadhay on the sets of a film titled *Autograph*. A lanky young man with thick glasses who was hanging around came up to me and introduced himself when he came to know that I was filmmaker Anurag Sen.

'I am Anupam,' he introduced himself, 'Anupam Ray.'

Anupam Ray was an amicable young man. 'I am a songwriter and singer,' he said. But then my agent enlightened me, 'He is an Electronics engineer, a gold medalist from the famous Jadavpur University. He has quit his high paying job with a multinational to chase his dreams.' There are very few people in this world who can follow their hearts. I remembered a classmate of mine who used to get highest marks in English and always dreamt of becoming a writer but later went on to work with some electrical equipment manufacturing company and sold transformers. I had met him once on board an Emperor Air flight and asked him about his writing. He had replied that it had died its natural death. 'You cannot write on an empty stomach pal; my life now revolves around only one thought as to how much discount I can offer on the transformer that my customer is looking for so that he buys it from me and not from a rival company and I can pocket my commission,' he had replied with a sigh.

I shook the hands of this young man Anupam Ray and wished him all the very best. Little did I know then that in a few days' time, he would be a celebrity giving the biggest Bengali hit song in many years – '*Amake, amar moton thhakte dao, ami nijeke nijer moton guchhiey niyechhi, jeta chhilona, chhilona seta na paoai thhak, sab pele nosto jiban…*'Let me live on my own, I've arranged my life in my way; what I didn't get, let it be; life is a waste if you get everything…'

'Wow what lyrics!' I couldn't help wondering how he got those lines that were so touching and so very soulful.'

After I had heard this song, I had decided that the next songwriter for my film would be him. I had called him up to ask if he could write in Hindi as well.

'Sure, I stayed out of Bengal for a long time,' he had replied. 'Why don't we meet some day?' he suggested, and I had agreed instantly. We met in flat of one of his friends, Srijit Mukherjee, who himself was a celebrated director. We discussed movies and music that evening and I had never found myself so enriched. I realised how deeply I loved the profession of filmmaking.

My next feature film with Prosenjit in the lead role as a cranky detective and Anupam Ray's music went on to a big hit again. I'll reveal more of that in the next book, as I had promised you readers earlier.

*****

6

TUM SAATH HO JAB APNE DUNIYA
KO DIKHA DENGE...

In a few days of my reuniting with Urmi, I took a decision that something had to be done about Anurit's disability. I enquired about good doctors in Calcutta and managed to fix an appointment with one of the most renowned neurosurgeons, one Dr. Rohan Kumar.

I was told to wait in the lounge attached to Dr. Rohan Kumar's chamber by the receptionist. I seated myself on the sofa set and picked up a copy of a few weeks old Stardust that had a photograph of Soma on the cover. 'Most promising newcomer,' the headline of the cover story said. Inside they had covered my movie, *Jeevan Ke Safar*, in quite detail and were all praise for me. I felt good indeed. There was no photograph of me though. But then how many directors' photographs do you see in film magazines? Actors are certainly the selling point of any film, and naturally audiences relate more with them than directors. I remembered an instance narrated by one of the most revered Bengali actors of all time, Soumitro Chattopadhay,. He had said that at one point in time, wearing *kurta* over trousers became a raging fashion statement of all Bengali youths (it still remains so, only that jeans have taken over trousers) and it all started after he had dressed in that attire in the movie, *Aranyer Din Ratri* (Day and Night of the Forest). But the entire concept was that of Satyajit Ray's, who was the director of the movie and needs no introduction. 'But everyone thinks, Soumitro Chattopadhay had started it all,' the veteran thespian had said smilingly.

My chain of thoughts was broken by the call of the receptionist, 'Your turn, Sir.' I got up and entered the doctor's chamber, where I had another surprise in store for me. On the side desk there was a framed photograph of a married couple, the groom of course was the doctor, and the bride's face seemed very familiar. I looked at it closely, as the doctor queried the reason for my seeking an appointment with him. But instead of answering him, I started off with a question,

'Are you Rittika's husband?'

The doctor was a tad bit puzzled, but then when I told him how I came to know Rittika, he lifted the receiver of the phone on his table and spoke, 'I am bringing someone for dinner.' He didn't pay any heed to my feeble protests suggesting visiting his house on a later date. He wanted to cancel all his appointments that day and leave for home with me, but I somehow prevented that and waited for him to finish seeing the remaining patients.

'I have heard a lot about you from Rittika,' he said and I told him about Anurit's medical condition on the way to his house. It was a big surprise for Rittika, for she had never expected me. She thought that her husband was bringing home some doctor friend of his. As Rittika chatted with me like a schoolgirl, in spite of her twin sons keeping her busy with their homework queries and she having to supervise the dinner preparations as well. They lived in a big house and she kept lamenting the dearth of trustworthy and capable maid-servants for its upkeep.

'Ah, you've become a perfect homemaker,' I had commented, for no housewife's talk could be complete without some maid-servant bashing.

'You know, whatever I do, I try to bring perfection in that,' she had replied with a chuckle. However, she kept regretting the fact that she had totally lost contact with me after her marriage.

Dr. Rohan Kumar went through Anurit's medical reports thoroughly, and said, 'It's a complicated case, but certainly the boy can be cured. I'll refer you to one Dr. Kramer, a renowned doctor from Switzerland who as a matter of great coincidence is now visiting Calcutta and is considered to be the final authority on this type of spinal cord deformity.'

Dr. Rohan Kumar arranged for an appointment with Dr. Kramer. It wasn't easy to get an appointment with a world-famous doctor just like that, but he couldn't quite say no to Dr. Mohan Kumar, who himself had a good reputation. I thanked him profusely and he confessed, 'Well, honestly I wouldn't have done so much for someone whom I don't really know had it not been for the fact that you are Rittika's friend.'

That evening, sitting alone, I wondered if there was anyone up there who decided it all. I remembered the day I first met Rittika. It was a coincidence of sorts, and now that it was only because of my friendship with her that Anurit's treatment could proceed under the supervision of such a famous doctor.

A few days later when Urmi had left for school, I took Anurit out on the pretext of taking him for lunch followed by a movie. While cinema and lunch was there on the agenda, I also wanted him to be checked by Dr. Kramer. I expected Anurit to throw tantrums while entering Fortis Hospital, but much to my surprise and relief, he kept absolutely quiet.

'We'll just meet a doctor and then go for lunch and movie,' I said.

'Sure,' he replied.

But the examination took far longer than I had envisaged, and when we came out, it was quite late. Dr. Kramer had declared after the check-up shuffling Anurit's hair, 'A minor operation and you can count yourself in the next World Cup football team.' He suggested that we go to Switzerland for the operation. 'We have a specialised team there,' he added.

After we came out of the hospital Anurit said, 'Let's skip the movie, and have a quick bite at a nearby McDonalds. It's already late, and we'll have to go back before Ma comes back.'

'OK,' I said admitting silently that the boy was very intelligent and mature for his age.

But that day Urmi had come back earlier, and when we went back, I expected a barrage of rebukes from her for taking Anurit out, but she didn't do anything of that sort. Over evening tea, I told her about what Dr. Kramer had said.

'But that will require a lot of money,' Urmi sighed.

'I can afford that now,' I said.

Urmi nodded in disapproval, 'It won't be nice to take money from you, and after all, we are just friends now, not into any deeper relationship.'

But the 'deeper relationship' happened in a few days' time.

One of the days shortly afterwards, Urmi and I were going past New Alipore where I stayed. We had been out to get some medical reports of Anurit from a hospital in the vicinity. With Anurit in the care of Masi, we were quite relaxed, when Urmi said, 'You are staying close by, isn't it?'

'Yes,' I said, 'a rented serviced apartment, as good as a hotel room at fraction of cost.'

'No, I wasn't asking about that, but in case you are living totally alone, can we drop in for a while, I needed to use the toilet,' she said.

'Oh! Of course,' I said, glad about the fact that she was becoming her old self again in my company.

I unlocked the room, and ushered her into a well-furnished but disheveled room. She went into the toilet, as I tried to arrange things a bit.

She came out in a while, with droplets of water still clinging to her face. As if by habit, she picked up the clothes that were lying on the chair, folded them and opened the wardrobe to look out for a hanger.

'Why didn't you get married?' she asked with her back turned towards me.

'May be I didn't get anyone like you,' my reply was spontaneous.

'You loved me that much?' she asked, hooking the hanger on to a rod.

I looked at her from back. She looked sexy in saree, her bottom had become fuller but she retained the same attractive figure. I craved to hug her from behind, an urge that I somehow overcame. Things had just started falling in place, I couldn't let it all go with a wrong move.

I kept quiet. I didn't know what to say. I loved her, but not that much. I loved her even more. She turned around, came close to me and planted a deep kiss on my lips. It was sudden, and it swept me off my feet.

It opened the floodgates, and the pent up passions exploded like a cloud burst. My mouth stuck on hers. She opened her mouth wide, hunger of a different kind evident from her craving. I felt an electric sensation surging through my body. We pressed against one another.

We came close, closer. Off came the clothes, one by one. I paused as she took off her bra and then her panties to gaze at the marvel that she exposed. I hugged her tightly to feel her nakedness all over me.

'V2 speed,' I thought, the speed at which the pilot cannot abort a take-off, but has to get airborne come what may, ignoring all the warnings. The slight deviation in focus at that point in time provided the necessary impetus to save me from messing up things that very moment.

She gripped my arms. Her nails tore into me. We were in flames. I could feel the sweat on her bare back dripping down as my hand followed. I sucked her inviting nipples like a hungry baby, gently squeezed her spongy buttocks, as she moaned hysterically. It was then time for the act to reach its natural ending.

Then - a moment before - inside, I kept very still. Our bodies moved in their own rhythm. Urmi's secret passage was swallowing, absorbing all that was mine to give. For those final moments, we united seamlessly - all the bitter memories of the past were negated by a common desire over which we had no control.

We remained still entangled for an eternity that seemed to be a fraction of a second. Urmi realised that it was getting very late. We dressed up quickly, as an ineffable feeling of joy swept all over me.

On the way back, Urmi gave her consent over going to Switzerland for Anurit's treatment.

⅋

'Hi Mote,' I had called him the next day.

'Oh Guru,' he yelled. Thereafter he went into details of the new fares on the menu of Roominos, and that the chili stuffed *samosas* were selling over 10,000 pieces a day. 'Oh!' I thought, 'The antacid makers must be making a killing by selling Pudin Hara and Eno then,' but went on to the important information that I wanted to convey. 'Mote, listen,' I said, 'We are going to Switzerland for Anurit's treatment.' It didn't take any time for him to understand for he was already aware of Anurit's medical condition.

'Guru, I'll make all arrangements,' he assured me, 'leave everything about your travel arrangements to me. I have a close friend who's a travel agent.'

'That's the good part to be a businessman,' I thought, 'you have friends at all the right places.' Mote overruled my feeble protest that I would be able to do the travel arrangements by myself. And all I had to do thereafter, besides visiting the embassy one day for the visas, was to get the printouts of the tickets and hotel bookings from the HP printer connected to Anurit's computer.

We left for Switzerland in a few days by an Emirates flight that flew to Zurich from Calcutta via Dubai. In spite of my insistence, Urmi didn't agree for the shopping stopover at Dubai on our way to Switzerland, nor did she agree to fly business class and so we were huddled in a 3-in-a row seat block. Though, in spite of Emirate's superb service, it was quite a struggle to travel sitting that way for 14 hours or so. I, of course, having being seated on the aisle seat, with Urmi occupying the middle one and Anurit the one beside the window got up often to unwind.

When the aircraft halted at Dubai, mesmerised by the glittering airport, Anurit said, 'We could have stopped over at Dubai, Ma.' 'On our way back, may be,' she told me pensively, 'if everything goes alright.'

I could gauge her anxiety. Yes, it was foolish on my part to talk of shopping in Dubai then. But our connecting flight was scheduled shortly thereafter and we left Dubai behind for another time. We landed at Zurich International Airport after a few hours.

Switzerland welcomed us with open arms. Mote had already booked a convertible BMW for our journey to the hospital from the airport. 'Self-drive or chauffer driven?' The man at the Hertz counter queried.

'Self-drive,' I said. Urmi looked at me skeptically and asked, 'Can you do that?'

'Of course,' I replied having gotten all the information from a friend of Mote who had lived in Switzerland for a long time, as I hauled the luggage into the expansive dickey of the fabulous car. We left Zurich behind quickly and drove into the countryside. Indeed, driving in Switzerland was an exhilarating experience with beautiful roads and fantastic scenic beauty. With the GPS screen guiding me, I didn't have any difficulties in finding the way too.

I couldn't help humming a few lines from the Amitabh-Vinod Mehra starrer Bemisaal, '*Kitani Khubsuraat yeh tasvir hain, mausam bemisaal, be nazir hain, yeh Switzerland hain, yeh Switzerland hain.*' Anurit clapped in glee, and Urmi broke into laughter. The out of tune song in my gruff voice was certainly worth it.

The hospital was located on the foothills of Mount Rigi, facing the Lake Laurez. It was perhaps one of the most beautiful places on earth. They quickly admitted Anurit, and a white flowing bearded doctor resembling Professor Albus Dumbledore of Harry Potter movies introduced himself to us as the director of the hospital. 'I am Professor Smitz, but you can call me Professor Dumbledore if you like,' he told Anurit, much to the amusement of all of us.

The operation wasn't as simple as Dr. Kramer had said. The six hours we waited outside the operation theatre felt like eternity. Urmi tried to look away from me, outside the huge glass window, focusing her gaze into the blue firmament, the lush green valley with countless flowers that set a riot of colours over it and the silent mountain peak. I too tried to get lost in the brilliance of the day, embosoming a calm cool vision of picture perfect scenery, in my desperation to drive away the anxiety that was clouding my mind. I focused my attention to the shards of sunlight percolating through the maze of gaps formed by leaves of tall trees creating patterns of shadows on the carpet of dark green grass. When I turned my gaze towards Urmi. I could see the reflection of her sad face with moist eyes, on the glass. I mustered courage to go near her and place my hand on her shoulder. She didn't move away but came closer and then she turned around and looked up to me and said, 'Sorry.'

'Sorry?' I wondered why she said so. But I didn't say anything. I searched my memory for an appropriate line to start a conversation, but could not. The wait was however over, as we were startled by Dr. Kramer's announcement from behind, 'Everything went on fine. He will start playing football in a week's time.' I held his hand in gratitude, and stupidly said, 'You must be very fond of football.' That ignited his passion for the game as he chatted for a quarter of an hour about his hopes of Switzerland making it into at least the quarter finals of the 2014 FIFA World Cup.

However, we were not allowed to see Anurit till the next day, when Professor Smitz came to me and said, 'Your son is fine.'

In my excitement, I mumbled and replied, 'Not my son, hers', and pointed to Urmi who had then just come out of the ladies restroom at the far corner of the corridor.

But Professor Smitz's reaction stunned me. He suddenly got very angry and almost howled at me, 'How can you deny that he is your son?' He then grabbed my neck and pushed me down the corridor to his office. He tapped on the computer keyboard and the printer spewed a report. He handed it over to me and said, 'Can't you see that your DNA and the boy's DNA match?' I remembered then that they had taken blood samples of both Urmi and me in case they required a transfusion. I took the report and mumbled in a choked voice, 'Thank you doctor,' and rushed out of the room.

Urmi was standing on the far corner of the corridor, alone, lost in her own thoughts. I ran to her as a nurse emerged from an adjacent door and called us, 'You can now see your son.'

We went inside the room where Anurit was sitting upright on his bed. 'Hi Ma, hi Papa,' he said and looking at Urmi's curious face added, 'I know Ma, Professor Dumbledore has told me all.' Urmi ran to her son, hugged him tightly and started sobbing. My eyes moistened as I was overcome with a plethora of emotions, 'Oh! Anurit is my son.' I wondered why then Urmi didn't marry me. Women are really very unpredictable, very very enigmatic. Perhaps that's why they make interesting company, but that kills you at times.

There was an atmosphere of celebration with the news of Anurit's operation being successful, but we were stunned by what happened next. Two nurses tried to make Anurit stand on his own. But as soon as they let him go, he fell on the floor writhing as if in great pain. Urmi bent down to assist him and so did I. I sighed, Urmi screamed. The operation wasn't successful we guessed. The doctors rushed in as the nurses talked among themselves, 'Dr. Kramer had never failed before.' They put Anurit back on the bed as the doctors started another round of check-up. Urmi and I moved away into the corridor. Both of us looked out of the huge glass window.

I asked her, 'Anurit is my son. Then why did you do that to me?'

She said in a choking voice, 'You weren't ready for marriage, and I wanted to have your son. I didn't want him to be born a bastard. I wanted a father's name for him. When you got the job, my marriage was already fixed; I just couldn't walk off like that distressing my parents. I should have done so. It was the biggest mistake of my life.'

I stood silently, not knowing what to say and got so lost in thoughts that I got oblivious of my surroundings. I was somewhat awakened by a tap from back. As I turned around, I saw Anurit standing behind me with a mischievous smile. Then I saw Dr. Kramer come out of a room with a football in hand. He rolled it towards Anurit who kicked it feebly.

I picked him up and held him high as Urmi joined in to hug both of us.

'How was the acting Papa?' Anurit winked at me and said, 'How about a *Taare Zameen Par* remake with me in the lead?'

'Oh what a son you've given me,' I turned to Urmi and yelled in mock anger. Urmi smiled even when her eyes were filled with tears. I felt that I had waited my entire life for this magical moment. Anurit hugged us tightly and whispered, 'Thank you; you've lighted up my life with THE JADOO OF YOUR LOVE!'

As we stayed in tight embrace with each other, everyone in the hospital – the doctors, nurses, the patients and all the other staff starting clapping in applause.

*****

EPILOGUE

When I went to meet Anurag Sen, to let him go through the final manuscript, he gave me an envelope.

'What is it?' I asked him.

'See for yourself.' He said.

I took out the letter inside and read it. It was a communication from Emperor Air. It said that Anurag Sen had been exonerated of all charges and he was advised to join duties at the earliest. It also said that his resignation had not been accepted, and that he was a very valuable employee of the company.

'Some postal glitch I suppose, delivering a letter after twelve years,' I said.

'No, the letter is not that old, issued some ten days back,' he said.

'Oh! Emperor Air is really fast in resolving disciplinary cases of employees,' I said sarcastically as coincidentally some Director of Emperor Air bragged about improved 'on-time performance,' on a business channel on the large screen TV set that was affixed on the wall of Anurag Sen's drawing room.

Anurag Sen threw the letter into a waste-paper basket as Urmi Sen (well, they got married in a simple ceremony immediately upon their return from Switzerland) came in the room with steaming hot tea and biscuits on a tray. Sipping on to flavoured Darjeeling tea, I insisted that Anurag Sen check the manuscript but he replied, 'Don't bother about that, your editing is good enough, go ahead with the publishing.'

As I was leaving, he asked me, 'Have you thought anything about your next novel?'

'Your filmdom stories as you have said earlier,' I said.

'Well, in that case, to begin with, I'll send you to a girl who was born in a brothel and went on to become a top heroine with her talent,' he said going into a pensive mood.

I didn't say anything, but the prospects of a writing a tinsel town story excited me. I hope to start working on it soon.

-Author